The King's Diamond

The King's Diamond

by
Lillian Harvey

UNITED STATES ADDRESS
Harvey Christian Publishers, Inc.
449, Hackett Pike, Richmond, KY 40495
Tel./Fax (423) 768-2297
E-mail: books@harveycp.com
http://www.harveycp.com

BRITISH ADDRESS
Harvey Christian Publishers UK
11 Chapel Lane, Kingsley Holt
Stoke-on-Trent, ST10 2BG
Tel./Fax (01538) 756391
E-mail: jjcook@mac.com

Printed in USA
First Edition 1963
This Edition 2014

ISBN: 978-1-932774-06-1

Cover Design by
Isaac Samuel
faithgrafikdesigns@gmail.com

Printed by
Lightning Source
La Vergne, TN 37086

Contents

"And they shall be mine, saith the Lord of Hosts, in that day when I make up my jewels."—**Malachi 3:17.**

CHAPTER ONE

IN SEARCH OF DIAMONDS

"I'm disillusioned, Ruth. I've mingled with multitudes of human beings, hoping to find human diamonds. They all prove common ore upon closer observation. How do you get rid of an angry sense of frustration?" Glyn asked me moodily as I came and took my place beside him. "You've an older head, and peace of heart that shows on your face," he went on. Give me the benefit of your experience. How do you get rid of frustration?"

"I wouldn't have thought that you had any reason for grousing," I replied as I studied this rare specimen of a cousin who had come so recently to visit us. It was a hot July day, and he had divested himself of his sports jacket which hung on a branch nearby. His expensive silk shirt had its sleeves rolled up well above the elbow, revealing muscular arms. It was evident my cousin was relaxing here in our orchard as he gazed dreamily at the running brook nearby.

Glyn Forster had a pleasing countenance. Some may not have actually called him handsome, but his intelligent brow revealed depths of thought, and his clean, refined appearance drew me irresistibly to this young man who, although a second cousin, was a comparative stranger. Many years had elapsed since I had seen him, and he was now representing his father's diamond interests in London.

"So you think you've mined all earth's human possibilities at the age of twenty-five?" I asked. "The world is large, and your search has perhaps been difficult so that you might be able to truly appreciate value when you do make the discovery. We lightly appraise what is easily secured."

His lips curled cynically. "I've been bitterly disappointed too often to retain any fond hopes for this rustic part of the world. I only wanted a quiet spot to which to come—away from the whirl of the city and its social demands—to think out my future. It was so good of you to invite me."

"One finds some of the rarest gems in the most unusual and out-of-the way places," I reminded him. "You see, since you've come, I've been reading up on diamonds. Wasn't the 'Star of South Africa,' that eighty-three-and-a-half carat stone, found in the possession of a Griqua witch doctor?"

"That's the story, but have you heard about the Cullinan diamond? Wells, the manager of mines near Johannesburg, was walking around the pit one afternoon when he noticed something glistening in the sun, high up on the wall of the crater near the surface. Climbing up, he dug out a blue-white diamond with his pen knife. It was as large as his fist and weighed 3,024 carats. Wasn't that a lovely stone to set before a king? It was presented to King Edward VII who had it cut into nine stones, the biggest of which was set in the royal scepter. Take a look at it sometime when you're in London."

"Better get your pen knife ready," I suggested. "You've been expecting to turn over tons of soil without success. It may be you, too, will see one glistening in the sun while you are on one of your walks."

He nodded gloomily and spoke as if to himself. "Life's funny. Take a chap like myself—money, education, best of family connections, and yet I'm as dissatisfied a fellow as you could find the world over. I don't seem to discover the kind of people I'm looking for.

"It all began with my old nanny," he continued. "I really blame her for this big overdose of discontent. I loved her dearly. Sitting on her knee or on a stool at her feet, I would listen spellbound as she related stories to me, whose characters glowed with strength and beauty. Narrations from the Bible were recounted in such a way that they still live to me. I believed I would go out and find such people in real life, but they only shine in story books. Then, I had a good headmaster whose lectures strongly influenced my young life, causing me to aim high. However, my quest for such persons in most circles has failed, and at the university I was taught that the Bible is only a compilation of myths and legends. We modern youngsters would say nanny and the head-master were a couple of 'squares.'"

He sighed and leaned his back on the trunk of the old pear tree which shaded us from the hot July sun. He nervously plucked a long piece of grass and then flung it from him impetuously.

"You've a delightful chapter ahead of you," I declared, trying to awaken his enthusiasm. "I know of some diamondiferous soil right here in this district which I shall have great delight in showing you. You have perhaps not been staking your claim in the kingdom of righteousness."

"Perhaps not. I'd never thought I could have been looking in the wrong places, but I'm setting up no more hopes only to have them dashed," he blurted out.

I rose saying, "I really came here to tell you that tea would be ready in thirty minutes. Are you hungry?"

"Your good country air has wakened my appetite," he admitted as he slowly straightened up his six feet of manhood and reached for his jacket.

"We've a few minutes yet. I want you to see the beauty spot on our grounds. It's just a slight climb; you aren't so gaunt with hunger that you can't take that, are you?" I questioned, pointing to the ascent.

"Not when I've been blessed with two long legs like these," he said, striding out. "I've enjoyed mountain climbing in more ways than one, and the effort is always amply repaid by the breath-taking view."

"So you've excavated for diamonds and climbed for views," I mused. "I've learned some valuable bits of information about you. I, too, have had some experience in the same pursuits."

"We ought to have a great deal in common, Ruth," he declared as he critically eyed me from head to foot. His eyes fell upon a woman of thirty-eight who still prided herself on her youthful outlook.

We had reached the summit and I stood slightly aside to watch his reactions. I had often arrived at conclusions about newly-found friends on this spot, which have proved to be true upon closer acquaintance. Nestled below, lay the lake with the quiet hills enclosing it and casting their reflections on its clear, mirror-like surface. Would he casually glance to satisfy propriety and then turn to speak of cars, women, or yachts? I wanted to take his measure and this was one of my yard-sticks. He made a picture as he stood there under the low-hanging copper beach boughs. With one foot on the low stone wall, and his elbow resting on his knee, he gazed first to right and then to left, drinking in the quiet beauty.

"I believe if I were here long enough I could shake off some of the bitterness and discontent," he said at last. "This beats the orchard and the brook."

"I thought you would love it," I responded. "I come here for my inspirations for an article, but often, too, I have received strength for the battle of life."

But if he had heard me he did not reply. He was letting the silence and calm of this place steal over him. I touched him on the elbow, "Have you forgotten you were hungry?" I reminded him. "I'm sure Jan will be waiting for us."

We walked slowly down the stone steps and the smooth, grassy slope to the neatly mown lawn, and the ancient trees, spreading out their branches, seemed to embrace us in their fatherly arms. The peace of the old, old house settled down upon us as we neared the entrance.

"It's a house with character," Glyn said as we approached.

"The peace of the old Quakers who built it still seems to guard its walls to this day," I explained. Dear father stood waiting in the doorway to welcome us. His snowy white hair, framing a face that the peace of God had molded into beauty, gave him a dignity which even ill-health and arthritis had not been able to deny him. A retired schoolmaster, father still felt at home among the youth, so it was a hearty welcome he gave to Glyn.

During the next few days I found Glyn a delightful conversationalist, well-informed and decided in his opinions. He found a place in father's heart as he seemed to guess his needs and so naturally and casually to fulfill them. Often long conversations would be carried on between them.

Knowing Glyn had come for quiet, we did not care to introduce him immediately to our village friends. I had hoped that Dr. Burns or Lois Stanford would have been among the first he would meet. They usually dropped in every few days, but news was quick to travel in a small village, and these were not the kind to intrude even upon the best of friends when they had guests.

It would happen, therefore, that we were not at first favored with the most polished specimens of the inhabitants of our district. Miss Lydia Scunthorpe and Mrs. Ainton called in one evening. Glyn, too, happened to be in. It was my usual task to hearten Mrs. Ainton, and console Miss Scunthorpe. Mrs. Ainton sat, the picture of despair, talking dolefully about these "last days that were right upon us."

"Reading the newspapers now-a-days makes one fear and quake. What with atoms, sputniks and all these rumors of war! Kruschev must be the beast with the ten horns. Don't you think so?" she enquired.

Miss Lydia sat bolt upright, twisting her hands as she acquiesced with her quaint, "Yes, yes," to all Mrs. Ainton said. "Ah me, ah me! Religion isn't what it used to be," and she sighed deeply. Her little bit of graying hair was tightly screwed into a knot on top of her head and stray wisps stuck out at right angles as if to add their protest to the deplorable state of things.

"Lydia and me's been discussing the number 666," she went on. "And ain't it dreadful the conditions of the young today. The place of worship ain't attended no more like it used to be."

Lydia responded by shaking her head violently and twisting her hands as she repeated her favorite lament, "Ah me, ah me! Religion isn't what—."

But a knock at the door interrupted the conversation, and I admitted Mr. Cheedle. Somehow I always dreaded his visits; now what would he say and do before my cousin? Although good at heart, one had to know him to understand. As usual, he breezed in as if he were joint owner of "Mountain View." Striking his hands together, he rubbed them vociferously as he proceeded to greet us all. His eye caught Glyn's, and I held my breath, wondering how this tactless guest of mine would speak.

"Brother," he said and he laid a heavy hand on Glyn's shoulder, "Do you love the Lord Jesus Christ? Would you be ready to die tonight?"

I answered for Glyn. "He is a cousin of mine, Mr. Cheedle. We are hoping his stay with us will help him in every way."

But Brother Cheedle was eyeing Glyn from head to foot. He finally turned his attention to the two women. "Say, Sisters, how about a wee time 'round the Bible. I've just had some interesting times with old Abraham scaring away the birds from his sacrifice."

"I am sorry, Mr. Cheedle," I interrupted. "I have just given orders for Jan to serve us some tea, and I think she has everything in readiness."

"Oh dear! Oh dear!" he muttered fretfully. "What's tea when we've the Bread of Life before us? 'We have meat to eat . . . '" he went on. But I was used to Brother Cheedle and knew that he would do justice to the refreshments better than any of us.

Glyn excused himself after tea and went out. Before my guests had left, Brother Cheedle had exhorted us all to scare away the birds of prey from our sacrifice. Mrs. Ainton was sure the birds of prey were portents of coming disaster, and Miss Lydia added her usual lament. Brother Cheedle prayed around the world and before he left, warned me that I must inform Glyn of his undone condition and make it uncomfortable for him. I kindly asked for Harry and Arthur, his two boys. Mr. Cheedle always became silent when this subject was mentioned, for his two sons were sowing some big fields of wild oats in our district.

Glyn stood in the doorway with a mischievous look after my guests had gone. "Is this the beginning of the new chapter in my diamond quest? Which is the 'Star of South Africa'?" and he chuckled heartily.

"They are hard to classify, Glyn, but they are really good at heart. I might explain it all like this: Not all the children who go to school could be termed scholars. Many just don't apply what they have learned to their daily lives. It's the same with professing Christians. Many take the initial step and with a mental assent accept the Lord Jesus as their Savior, but they never dream of applying His teachings and commands to their daily lives. I think my diamonds are those who have crowned Christ Lord, and so apply His teachings to all their actions. They learn the lessons of self-denial, cross-bearing, and suffering well in this School of Christ, and they never finish their education, because they are always taking honors and acquiring more knowledge. You will never question my diamonds once you have met them. With these—well, we must patiently seek to lead them higher."

"They are at least individuals," Glyn admitted, "but when do I meet diamonds?"

"Tomorrow afternoon, if you like. I always visit Mrs. Stanford several times a week. Though an invalid, she is a happy, contented woman."

"Perhaps she has something to make her content," he protested tartly.

"You shall judge for yourself. She's a confirmed invalid as well as a widow, having lost a wonderful husband. She has experienced since then the constant pinch of poverty, and has known other poignant sorrows. She's one of my diamonds."

"There must be a snag somewhere. How long have you known her?"

"Twenty years," I explained, "and that is surely long enough to test a character and watch it in the process of polishing. She'd love to meet you, and I think . . . yes, I know she will remind you of your nanny and headmaster."

*** *** * * * * * *

I didn't know whether Glyn would accompany me, but he was ready, faultless in appearance and with a basket of fruit. "I'm almost afraid to meet one of your diamonds. I'm an expert at detecting flaws or 'inclusion,' as we would call it in business language. I don't want to disillusion you."

"My diamonds will stand your tests. I rather welcome an expert's examination. They may need a great deal more polishing, but they are rare diamonds," I asserted confidently as we walked along winding roads. A slight mist covered us, giving a rather welcome though temporary protection from the already sultry July heat. I had not told him of the second diamond—I was anxious for him to meet the two. But was he an expert? I wondered if his worldly background and materialistic viewpoint is the right magnifying glass with which to detect true jewels.

As we neared their cottage, trimmed in black and white paint, the sun broke through the mist, giving us as beautiful a view of "Sunny Mount" as I had ever had. Nature had befriended the old house, for rambler roses were at their best and climbed so confidentially up the walls and around the windows that the cottage seemed in its greatest glory. Nature, the decorator, had taken over, covering its plain walls with her handiwork.

As we stood at the garden gate I saw Glyn was reading the little wooden sign held by two garden elves: "One is near to God's heart in the garden." And then, as we entered, we looked up to see one of my diamonds. She had not heard us enter and was busily engaged weeding a rose bed. She was singing:

> "I have given up the world for Jesus,
> Left its pleasures for the Christ of Calvary."

I did not wish to startle her, so we stood a moment taking it all in. Her clear, sweet voice continued:

> "I have given up the world for Jesus,
> Now He is all the world to me."

Then it was that she saw us, and her face crimsoned as she realized that her love song to Christ had been overheard.

"It was a song we had been practicing," she informed us smiling. "I thought I only had mother for my audience. Work goes faster when one sings."

Introductions were quickly made, and we followed Lois into the house and through to the bedroom where the invalid lay. Her bed had been pulled up as near the French window as possible. Rays of sunshine danced across the candlewick bedspread. The little pink roses at the window and in the vases matched those on the wallpaper. But, completing the picture, was the invalid woman herself, propped up with snowy-white pillows which guarded the aching back. On the bed lay her open Bible, and a well-stocked bookshelf was within easy reach.

"I've brought you a visitor." I informed her. "Meet Glyn Forster, my cousin, Mrs. Stanford."

"You've never told me about this cousin, Ruth," said the sick woman, extending her hand cordially.

"No, actually we are second cousins, and our lives have been lived in very different parts of the world so that we really have not known one another. Glyn's father has interests in the diamond fields in Africa, and he has had diamonds talked to him from babyhood. He doesn't believe, however, that in the world of humans there are any diamonds—or at least he thinks that there can be only very, very few. I thought you might help him."

Glyn laughed, but explained, "I have had a great deal to do with diamonds, and father's mines turn over a great deal of blue earth to find one diamond. But, I declare I've turned over tons and tons of human beings and I've not been very lucky. I've been successful in business, but I have to admit in human relations my ventures have been hopeless failures. I came to this quiet spot to think it all out and to study diamond prospecting in the sphere of human relationships."

Mrs. Stanford had been watching Glyn's face and I could tell that her motherly heart went out to this wealthy young man—so poor in the things in which she was rich and so rich in that in which she was so poor. "Glyn, I may call you that?" questioned Mrs. Stanford.

"Make it Glyn," he said heartily.

"We will do all we can to help you in your search for diamonds. I found some in Africa, too, while out with my good husband. I know the One Who takes worthless ore, and when He has finished, He has converted it into a diamond of amazing beauty. We found many black diamonds. But let us know just what you are looking for."

"It's useless, I tell you. They don't exist. You would only laugh at my high ideals. I never mention them any more to people because they think I'm eccentric."

"Laugh!" she repeated. "We should be very happy in this age of 'no standards in anything' to find some young person thoughtful enough to know what he wants and who will search until he finds! Let's hear about these qualities that make jewels, Glyn. I'm most interested, I can assure you," Mrs. Stanford affirmed sincerely.

"Well," Glynn began, "there are six outstanding characteristics of a diamond. I should like to find real, honest-to-goodness people who could stand the same tests our diamonds are put through.

"Number one. They are the hardest substance known, eighty-five times harder than any other known substance. I should like to discover persons who instead of being easily grooved by elements that contact them, would, instead, be hard enough to impress others. Popular opinion and dictates of fashion deeply groove most people, but my diamonds should be able to not only withstand this influence but to impress others instead.

"Number two. They are unspoiled by alkalis or acids. A true gem should be able to mix with the sordid business world, social circles, and centers of learning without contamination. How many come out unspoiled, unspotted, or untarnished by flatteries or frowns, praise, or blame?

"Number three. A diamond can stand intense heat and still be uninjured. Talk about a furnace of affliction! We can't stand an ordinary shift on a hot day without complaining. How easily people are turned aside from a purpose because of some adversity. A diamond can stand terrific heat and be unharmed.

"Number four. A diamond disperses light. This is an unusual quality, and is what makes this gem so beautiful. Taking light, which to the human eye looks white, it breaks it up and then disperses it in all the colors of the rainbow. Give me a human gem who can take the simple duties and pleasures of life, and, because of an inner quality of soul, make them appear more than simple—beautiful, glowing with all the colors of the rainbow.

"Number five. A diamond refracts. This, too, makes it beautiful. It has power to take light and bend it towards its center and then send it back out. I've put this test over and over again—invariably people take in light, but they don't bother sending it back out because they don't possess number six.

"Number six. A diamond is pure. If a diamond has what we call 'inclusion' it is rejected and used for industrial purposes. Only as a diamond is pure can it send the light back out in unspoiled beauty. Selfishness mars so many otherwise beautiful characters.

"The polishing I could trust to time," Glyn continued as he leaned back. He had been so intense that he had been sitting on the edge of his chair. "You've heard enough of me and my wants. I would like to hear about yourself and how you achieved the great art of being contented."

"My life has been so full of fascinating things that I don't know where to start," she replied.

"You call this fascinating—being an invalid? Dispersion—number four." The conversation was interrupted when Lois entered with a dainty tray and a cooling drink. I noticed Glyn studying my friends. Lois looked fresh and sweet in her newly laundered frock. It had been mended and was a last year's buy. Her lovely brown hair curled naturally around her face and was swept back loosely. Her face was beautiful because the bloom of youth was there, but Mrs. Stanford had a radiance upon her countenance which I knew had been attained through suffering and communion with Jesus Christ.

"I am interested in your secret of contentment. You were going to tell me how you achieved it," and Glyn set his glass down and looked curiously at Mrs. Stanford. "I've been to doctors, specialists, and psychologists to find out this secret."

Mrs. Stanford knew that her usual religious vocabulary would not be understood by this man of the world, so she asked silently for wisdom to simply shine out the Light of life in the wonderful hues with which He had appeared unto her.

"Perhaps I should start with my life in the days when I was not at all a contented or happy young woman, lest you believe I was born contented. My father was an architect and had succeeded in business. I was given all that should make a young woman happy—money, friends, education. My talents lent themselves to art, and I succeeded enough to gain praise from a famous master. Pleasure, balls, theaters, dances—all gave me a thrill of momentary pleasure, but, although I seemed the gayest of the gay, my heart ached with a discontent at night that seemed unbearable. The next morning, however, would find me outwardly the same carefree self.

"A very close chum of mine died suddenly and a new form of ache was added to my inner unrest. The thought of eternity haunted me. What if it had been I? At this juncture, I attended a religious service with another art student. The young preacher, dead in earnest, pictured my exact state until I felt most uncomfortable. It seemed as if someone had told him all about me. He vividly portrayed the aching void, the cover-up, the head-long plunge into something new—something always ahead and yet all ending with the same great inward discontent. I call it an ache for want of a better word.

"He spoke from that verse, 'She that liveth in pleasure is dead while she liveth.' He spoke of a wonderful life through Christ—of the need of a second birth. 'I am come that they might have life,' he said Jesus had promised. I thought I had life—now I knew it was only physical life. And as he spoke of the death of Christ upon the cross I saw that Eternal Life had been purchased for me."

Suddenly a spasm of pain passed over the face of the speaker, and she grew pale. Lois quickly re-arranged the pillows and Mrs. Stanford leaned back exhausted.

"Mother's spirit is stronger than her frame and has long beaten it unmercifully until Nature has rebelled and taken her toll," Lois explained. "She has overdone for today. I am sure you will not mind having the story continued another day, Mr. Forster?"

"Glyn," he corrected.

Turning to me, Lois said, "Mother would not like you to go without a word of prayer. I am sure your cousin would not object," she ventured as she looked to him. "It's a 'must' for mother."

Glyn bowed respectfully, and then we rose to go. Lois accompanied us to the gate and invited us back again. We walked slowly homewards in the sunshine. Would Glyn wish to return where so much of the conversation was about religion? We both seemed lost in thought. I had not wished to "push" religion at Glyn, and yet here, by his own request, he had given Mrs. Stanford the opportunity I had desired. Would he care to remain in these quiet, rustic surroundings?

"A penny for your thoughts," he said as we went along.

"Mine aren't up for sale at any price," I informed him. So we walked along the rest of the way in silence. I found that when unsolicited, Glyn spoke more freely. I hoped he would one day divulge his impressions of the visit, but I feared that money, elegance, and the maxims and customs of the world had so spoiled his taste for the more simple forms of happiness that he would be a poor judge.

I glanced at him as he advanced to open the gate leading to "Mountain View." His clothing was cut from the most expensive of materials and pressed to perfection. There was in his whole manner the self-possession that comes to one used to moving in circles of wealth and affluence. I thought, in contrast, of the pinch of poverty in the Stanford home that was bound to show itself in spite of the clever and tasteful way my friends had tried to conceal it. How did Glyn like my diamonds, I wondered?

CHAPTER TWO

DIAMOND TESTING

We were favored with special callers in the late afternoon of the following day. Audrey Castleton and Sheina Rayhurst drove up. I had expected them because you could be certain that wherever the limelight was focused upon Bradleholme, these two were sure to figure prominently in the picture. Audrey said they had come to discuss the coming session of the monthly social which she had initiated several years before.

Audrey was twenty-three and possessed an exceptionally brilliant mind, as well as a talent for organizing. She had roped in the entire community—that is, with the exception of Lois and myself. Closer acquaintance with Audrey revealed to me that she was a Miss Facing-Both-Ways. She was ever on the popular or winning side. If Christianity waxed strong, she deplored the shallowness of the times; if Christianity waned, she was ready to judge its votaries to be narrow and constricted. Most of the excellent people of Bradleholme, however, were unaware of Audrey's duplicity.

She had learned of my deep attachment to Lois and so was guarded in my presence. But one day I had entered the little Community Hall before the time expected. I overheard Audrey's voice saying, "Yes, Sheina and I were just remarking that Lois is a square. She really hinders progress here. We wonder what tiny niche in the world she could possibly fill—maybe an old-maid with her glasses like this, teaching piano lessons to our children in Bradleholme." There were peals of laughter, and so engaged were they all that they had not seen me as I had entered, nor did they see me as I turned in indignation and walked out of the hall.

As I stood on the doorstep, waiting for Lois to appear, everything made sense. Up to that time, Audrey had skillfully hidden her duplicity from me. She had always spoken to me of my friends in such a way as never to rouse my suspicion. Many memories now flooded my mind as I recalled scenes and events that helped me understand the constant state of misapprehension created in our little village. When Lois eventually joined me and we entered the building together, Audrey gave us a most enthusiastic welcome. She locked arms with Lois, whispering confidentially into her ears; onlookers would have thought them the best of friends.

One day, Lois came to me in great perplexity about Audrey. I had noticed a peculiar distance at times between these two, but we had never discussed Audrey together. Lois had known her since school days. Although three grades above her, Audrey's conduct was such as to convince Lois of her ability to play two games at once. Although a favorite of the teachers and a prefect, Audrey could ridicule the "silly old master" as well as the rules. But to the master she was dutiful, even flattering, telling him how she had admired the way in which he handled the undisciplined youth of today. Time after time Lois, in disgust, had watched Audrey play to the galleries. She couldn't tolerate her pretended intimate friendship when to her own advantage, so quickly followed by equally annoying ostracism and even ridicule with no apparent reason for the change.

Piqued at her inability to subdue this young woman four years her junior, Audrey was unable to understand Lois Stanford. Her self-assurance withered under truth's searching gaze and one day she lost her self-possession enough to blurt out, "Don't look at me that way. You make me feel like a child that's been naughty. Haven't you any sense of humor?"

Sheina Rayhurst was much more attractive in looks than Audrey, but she lacked the drive and forcefulness that the other possessed. She had a talent for public speaking and was also gifted along musical lines. The attachment between these two was very, very close. Had it not been for this hero-worship for Audrey, I could have found it in my heart to really love Sheina. I always believed it was a case of a weaker nature twining itself around the stronger, masterful one, rather than having any base motives such as actuated the other.

Now on this particular afternoon, there Audrey sat, so self-confident and yet so innocent-looking and so seemingly interested in the spiritual welfare of the district that I almost had misgivings as to my recent judgment.

"We heard that you had a very distinguished visitor," Audrey began. "It is really a most unusual event for Bradleholme to be so honored; but to come to the point, we were wondering if Mr. Forster could not speak at our coming meeting. I understand he knows a great deal about diamonds. Couldn't he give this rustic community a change from its usual Dr. Burns, Mr. Marchant sort of thing? I'm rather concerned and challenged over the unchurched youth, and thought this might be a golden opportunity of getting them under Christian influence."

"But Glyn, my cousin, doesn't profess to be a Christian," I revealed. "His talk would be purely educational—very excellent, doubtless—but if your interest is chiefly the spiritual welfare of the youth, I am afraid my cousin couldn't show them the way to Christ, for he doesn't know the way himself. He is a fine, moral character, but it ends there."

She had raised her eyebrows when I mentioned the word "cousin" and then remarked, "Couldn't you add the spiritual applications afterwards? The young folks take a lot from you as you have such a way with them."

"You will need to take the matter up with my cousin," I suggested. "He should be in any time now. He's a man of decision; I cannot make plans for him." Excusing myself, I hastened to arrange tea, but on returning found that the lounge was empty. I rang the gong to announce that refreshments had been prepared and soon Glynn and the two girls came in from the garden.

"We've managed to persuade Mr. Forster to speak next Saturday night," Audrey volunteered triumphantly.

An hour later, as we watched Audrey's car disappearing down the drive, Glyn commented wryly, "How she got me to promise that talk, I can't fathom. Before I knew it, she had even turned my refusal into polite acceptance. I say, she has a very brilliant mind and is well informed."

"She is a forceful and striking personality and usually does get her own way," I confessed.

Saturday night came, and the little Community Hall was filled to capacity. Audrey's talent for organizing was apparent in the smooth running of the program. Glyn's talk was exceptionally interesting and instructional and enabled me to better understand his search for diamonds. Since much diamond language is used in this story, I thought a brief synopsis of his talk would be enlightening.

GLYN'S LECTURE ON DIAMONDS

The African sun shone mercilessly upon Erasmus Stephanus Jocobs as he walked leisurely over the fields on an errand for his father. Sitting down under a tree to rest awhile, the lad noticed a glittering pebble lying nor far from him. Curious, he picked it up from where it had been lying, surrounded by limestone and ironstone. As he walked homewards toward the farm, little did Erasmus grasp the significance of his find; thousands of men would leave home and family to stake claims along the banks of the Orange River in order to search for these sparkling stones.

Arriving home, the boy gave the gem to his sister who put it with her playthings. One day they wanted to play a game known as "Five Stones," so the sparkling pebble was used as one of the five. A neighbor, Van Niekerk, arrived during the game, and attracted by the brilliant stone, it became his property, but it was not long before he had sold it for a few pounds to a peddler named O'Reilly. It was then sent to a mineralogist and eventually, as the real worth of the gem became known, there was a rush to stake claims and buy up farmsteads. The O'Reilly diamond was a twenty-one carat blue-white stone which was sold for something in the neighborhood of five hundred pounds.

Diamond mining thus began in real earnest in South Africa, and today well over ninety percent of the world's supply comes from this area. But as far back as 800 B.C. diamonds had been discovered along the riverbeds of India. South America also yielded some of these precious stones. For many, many years it was thought that they could only be found in river-beds or on land adjacent to river courses. More recently, diamonds have been mined from blue ground and at a depth of three thousand feet, which has greatly altered the methods used in securing them.

Why are diamonds so very costly? Because they are procured by infinite pains and labor. Four tons of soil must be mined in order to secure a one-carat diamond. There are 142 carats in just one ounce. Is it any wonder that these minute jewels are costly? In the famous

Kimberley mines, twenty-five million tons of earth were mined for only three tons of diamonds.

But how do they tell which is earth, gravel, pebble, or diamond? The earth is first crushed and the gravel is carried off to a plant outside the mine. Here the gravel is washed and sieved so that the smaller pieces sift through. The larger pieces are washed in a separate solution and then sent down sloping tables which have been coated with one-half inch of grease. As diamonds are water-repellent, they stick to this coat of grease, and afterwards the substance is scraped off the tables and melted. As the diamond can stand heat up to 1,600 degrees Fahrenheit the gems can be separated in this way.

To an untrained eye, a valuable diamond may be mistaken for just an ordinary piece of glass, as it is usually coated with a greasy substance which needs cleansing in an acid bath. They are afterwards sent to expert cutters. Under a microscope, any flaw or imperfection is noticed. If these are found to be serious, they are called inclusions, and the faulty stones are reserved for industrial purposes.

The cutter or polisher multiplies the value of a diamond from one hundred to two hundred times its original worth in the raw state. One pound of uncut diamonds in the rough is worth approximately four thousand pounds. By skilful cleavage and polishing, phenomenal results are obtained and the same weight in diamonds (one pound of one-carat diamonds), will bring anywhere from five hundred thousand pounds to eight hundred and thirty-three thousand pounds! You can see that the cutter and polisher are in great demand.

The diamond is the hardest known substance. At the beginning of diamond mining in South Africa, it was thought that the worth of the stone in question could be tested by subjecting it to hammer blows. Some precious gems were thus shattered, for it was not then known, that although a substance itself so hard that it could cut a groove in the hardest surface, it still could be shattered by the light tap of a hammer. Great care is therefore taken by the expert before dividing the stone into several smaller ones. Sometimes as much as two months' time is given to studying the gem before cleavage.

The real beauty of the diamond, however, is brought about by polishing facets upon its surface. This is done by a cast-iron disc which revolves at 2,500 revolutions per minute and is coated with diamond dust and olive oil. Being so hard a surface, it requires diamond dust to polish it. Imagine how very careful the expert must be to get each little facet at the right angle, the right size, and the right shape. Half of the stone will be lost in this beautifying process for the most expensive diamonds have fifty-eight facets. In its raw state, this gem has eight to twelve surfaces or facets. Amazing feats have been accomplished with small gems. One was once on exhibition no larger than a pin head, and yet this tiny jewel had fifty-eight facets polished upon its surface.

Although we are entranced by stories of large diamonds such as the Kohinoor, the Star of South Africa, the Jonker gem, the Cullinan diamond, it is really the smaller diamonds which make the trade profitable. Men lured by the vision of finding some large, beautiful gem, dig and mine and die—many times as poor as they began.

*** *** * * * * * *

Elsewhere in my story, I have given Glyn's description of the six points relative to the diamond, so will not go into detail again here. A question time followed. I had been tremendously impressed with the analogy between a redeemed soul and the diamond, but Audrey announced that our time was gone, so no spiritual applications were made. I had not expected it anyway.

At home, Glyn and I were enthusiastically discussing the diamond trade, when suddenly he changed the subject saying, "I've met clever young women in society, but it is unusual, I believe, to find superior mental qualities in Christian circles. Audrey and Sheina are really quite accomplished and able young women. Are they some of your diamonds?"

He was scrutinizing my face closely. "That is for the microscope to discover," I evasively reminded him. "You very aptly pictured tonight the processes of the expert's examination. I suggest you start applying these tests to Audrey and Sheina."

"I've already applied one test," he disclosed with a twinkle in his eye and he turned and left me, saying, "Good night." Glyn had a way of leaving me guessing, but that was why this cousin was so intriguing.

The following week, I was busily writing, up in the little summer house, when a shadow fell across my papers on the table. Glyn had avoided church on the Sunday and had been quite busy about his own business for the first few mornings of the week. In the afternoons he had been golfing or playing tennis with Audrey, Sheina, and several of their friends.

"Have you had anything in the way of refreshment, Glyn?"

"Well, I could eat by and by, but I've something on my mind I want to get off first," he ventured.

Glyn seated himself in the rustic chair opposite my work table. "I was into Glasham today and while walking around the market, whom do you think I saw?" He made his own reply so quickly that I had no opportunity to return an answer. "Lois Stanford was selling fruit and vegetables at a market stall! Have things reached such straits that a young woman like her need reduce herself to so common an occupation?" he questioned indignantly.

"Lois doesn't consider that to be lowering herself, Glyn," I observed. "Indeed, she has very decided views on the matter of what sullies. Father and I would have loved to have given financial help more than once, but the two daughters would have felt hurt. Our giving must be in very guarded and disguised ways."

"Hm-m-m, an independent tribe," retorted Glyn. "Are circumstances so reduced that she must sell garden produce to help make a living? I watched her chatting away to old ladies, and the poor seemed to draw out her sympathies. She appeared perfectly happy and contented in such surroundings."

"She is exactly that, Glyn. If you knew her as I do, you would know that Lois is truthful throughout—transparent and pure—wasn't that one of your points in assessing a diamond?"

"I do not know her as you do so I cannot comment," he replied archly. "But how can she improve her mind in such an environment?"

He was cynical, and I could not appreciate it. "Lois is studying Hebrew and Greek in her evenings under Dr. Burns' tutoring. You have only to converse with Lois to know what a superior mind she has and how well informed she is for a girl of nineteen. Next time you are in the home, glance over their book shelves and read the titles. She is acquainted with them all. If you attend church tomorrow, you shall hear her accomplishments in music for she is the organist and also renders solos when needed."

"Is there nowhere else to hear this very exceptional young woman with such unusual ability except at church? She did not render a musical item at the Community Hall the other night," he volunteered.

"Lois was not asked for her services that evening, but I doubt whether she would ever exhibit her musical talent for mere display or curiosity. If some elderly persons at the County Homes desired her services, she would rise to the occasion."

"So she is the bread-winner?" he queried curiously.

"She shares that load with an older sister. Carey is teaching at an elementary school and is only home for a week-end now and again. Their father died when Lois was fourteen and Carey seventeen. Carey went on and has procured a teaching certificate; Lois only managed to finish high school education passing the G.C.E. with flying colors. But Mrs. Stanford was taken ill and instead of the planned education being continued, she chose to remain at home and become both nurse and housekeeper. Her sister gives what she can from her salary after her own heavy expenses are deducted. I believe Mrs. Stanford had a considerable sum left her by her grandfather, but it was all given to help print the New Testament in the vernacular of the people among whom she and her husband had labored. She and her daughters take pleasure in knowing that they have benefited others with their financial resources. With that for a background, Lois does not feel at all ashamed of laboring with her hands to meet the family's present budget."

"But," Glyn questioned further, "isn't she much too young to be such a prisoner? She needs fun and plenty of companions. She will go stale and utterly stagnate in so confined a circle. Some people are good and pure only because they have not been subjected to temptation."

"Go stale! It is having no outlet that causes water to stagnate. Remember one of your six points was refraction—bending the light toward the center and then sending it back out. You complain of this very stagnation in acquaintances of yours who are constantly in the whirl of society, fun and pleasure—ever taking in, but never, never giving out. We, here in Bradleholme, know to whom we would like to go if we were in difficulty; we know who would freely give us a sympathetic hearing. As for temptations, Bradleholme has its imperious demands and troublesome people to try one's mettle."

"But she hasn't stood the greater temptation of the larger cities, and the glittering attractions of elite society. The flatteries one encounters there have spoiled most of the young women I know," Glyn replied.

"Remember the story of David? If one contends successfully with the lion and the bear in obscurity, one can hope to be successful with the giant Goliath on the wider battle-field of life. Tell me, did Lois recognize you in the market?" I enquired anxiously.

"No, I chose to keep at a distance. She was so occupied that I had a fair opportunity of studying your gem under most unusual circumstances. There was a young farmer who had a stall next to hers. They seemed on very friendly terms, and I suppose the market would be quite a good place to pick up an eligible young farmer for a husband," Glyn bantered.

"That's Joe Brunner and he often befriends the Stanfords by taking their produce to and from the market," I added, but here we were interrupted.

"Ruth, oh Ruth," Lois' voice rang out as she came up breathlessly after the climb. I could easily see her, but Glyn's chair had been pushed back into the corner and he chose to keep himself out of sight. She stood near the entrance of the door, flushed and excited.

"I can't stay, but I did want to tell you I had sold everything early today. Joe brought us back several bags of potatoes, too. I was able to buy mother that bed jacket I've been fondly viewing every week. She looks queenly in it, and is so pleased. I've been able to put another 10 shillings (half a pound sterling) towards treatment," she informed me. Suddenly, she became aware of Glyn's presence, and pushing her head round the corner, she met his amused glance. She blushed and laughed heartily.

"Glyn, why not tell Lois what was troubling you today?" I begged, as I pulled out a small stool and urged Lois to be seated.

"You were under close observation at Glasham today, young woman," Glyn said mischievously.

Lois tossed her head back as she remarked, "I don't think I did anything of which to be ashamed, even under close scrutiny, but what troubled you about my conduct, may I ask?"

"The occupation seems rather a degrading one for so accomplished a young woman as Ruth says you are," he replied. "Can you say you really like it?"

"I enjoy myself immensely. I would not choose it for my life's vocation, but under the circumstances, I try to extract the best. The market is a wonderful place for studying humanity. One finds oneself going through a university course in the school of life just studying faces and actions. If I ever am inclined to be disheartened, I repeat to myself a quotation by James Russell Lowell, 'After all, the kind of world one carries about in one's self is the important thing, and the world outside takes all its grace, color and value from that within.'"

"I see you need to bolster yourself up. You must have some misgivings at times?" he queried kindly.

"Well, unkind remarks reach my ears. I suppose we are all human enough to feel a bit cut up when we see people judging standards by outward appearances—dress, money, and the kind of work one does. I've determined to make them think stall-holding quite an elevated job before I'm finished," she asserted confidently.

"Lois," I interrupted, "do repeat that story of Epaminondas you were telling me about the other day."

"Well, my mother read it to me some time ago when things were going hard. Now, if she sees me feeling a bit down, she'll say, 'Remember Epaminondas!'"

"I might need to be reminded, too, so give it to us," Glyn urged.

"Epaminondas lived in the city of Thebes in ancient Greece," Lois began. Besides being a good general in time of war, he proved a great leader in peace. But there were those in power who became jealous. They plotted to nominate him at the next election to the job of keeping the streets clean, meaning to humiliate and lower him in the eyes of the citizens. To this post he was elected, and so well and conscientiously did he perform his duties that the post became honorable and one much sought-after in subsequent election."

"That's one to remember, Lois. But, honestly, you are a strange mixture. You are unabashed when I mention stall-holding. Most young women would be humiliated, but you proudly quote ancient history and modern writers to support your position. You completely silence me. You'll have me running for the job of stall-holding in the next elections," Glyn confessed good-humoredly.

Lois looked at her watch. "I must get back in time to prepare tea," she exclaimed. "I just popped in, Ruth, to tell you of my success." Nodding to Glyn, she said her "cheerio" and left us as abruptly as she had appeared.

"What do you think of my jewel?" I inquired.

"More close examinations to make—too early to comment," he informed me evasively.

*** *** * * * * * *

Sunday morning it was raining, and I did not think Glyn would care to attend our small church. But I found him dressed and standing waiting for me with his hands behind his back, looking out upon the garden which was being cleansed and refreshed by the cooling rain. As we both preferred walking, we put on our raincoats and stepped out into the slight drizzle.

"I didn't anticipate the pleasure of your company this morning," I admitted to Glyn as we walked down the long drive.

"It's something I haven't done for a long time," he confessed. "For years, I tried going to church faithfully every Sunday morning, but it seemed in my honest moments as if I were seeking an indulgence for the way I spent the remainder of the day," he confessed.

"You're at least honest. Did you never receive benefit?"

"I couldn't say I did. It seemed rather foolish for me to go to church if the Bible wasn't true. My conscience always troubled me. Psychologists said it was the result of religious inhibitions received in childhood, but while in Rome, I'll do as the Romans do. Most of Bradleholme, I imagine, turn out to church?" he questioned.

"Not all Bradleholme, but the godlessness of the large cities has not as yet engulfed us here. Our minister is evangelical and no modernist, but here we are at 'Sunny Mount,'" I explained. "We'll see if Lois has left yet."

Lois had already gone on ahead so we walked the rest of the way enveloped in our own thoughts. I was very proud of our little church. It stood back off the main road, and from its entrance one could watch the quiet ripples of the nearby lake chase each other to the shore. We entered and as we took our seats, the organ pealed out strains resounding like angel songs that would have to burst if they could not express, in some way, their imprisoned, pent-up adoration. God's peace and the calm of the Sabbath settled over me, and all that was sordid, mean, and fleeting seemed out of bounds in this atmosphere.

When Dick Marchant opened the vestry door and entered the pulpit, I thought he was a man of whom to be proud. He was twenty-seven and filling this out-of-the-way post while making his final preparations for going abroad. Abiding communion had left its trace upon his countenance. He was stockily built, and his shock of light curly hair made his face look almost boyish. All was forgotten, however, as he led the service, for he had an indefinable air of authority. By his faithfulness in visitation, he had endeared himself to the villagers, who responded by turning out to his services.

The congregation soon became infected by the earnestness of the minister, his choice of hymns, and his hearty singing, and his prayer was such that we felt we had actually been brought into the presence of the King, and that our petitions had been heard. Then Lois sang, at Dick Marchant's request, that familiar old hymn, "The Ninety and Nine." Such was the unaffectedness and sincerity of the singer that every word of that hymn seemed to be meaningful.

Dick's sermon was challenging to both Christian and unbeliever alike. It contained enough truth to save a seeking soul, I thought to myself, as we walked slowly down the aisle of the church at the close of the service. We waited outside the entrance for Lois, as she had been detained by Mr. Marchant. Glyn eyed her critically as she stood in the door-way talking animatedly to our young minister. Dressed in a neatly tailored costume with a little blue hat nestled comfortably in the center of her brown wavy hair, I thought she had never looked more attractive.

Audrey approached us and introduced several of her friends to Glyn. As usual, she was tastily dressed, but she had chosen a style in hair and dress so cautiously that she gave no offence to the ultra-fashionable, and yet kept within bounds in the eyes of the stricter church-members. Her vivacity and overflowing spirits, however, were her greatest attraction.

As Lois joined us and we walked homeward, Glyn seemed in a provocative mood, "Audrey's vivacity and push seem to make her the organizer in this district. Is that true?" he questioned as he directed his conversation to Lois.

"She does a great deal of organizing and does it efficiently, too," Lois replied quietly.

"What kind of work is she engaged in?" he asked.

"She handles some of the welfare work for this area and is expecting promotion soon to an even more trusted post, I believe, in London. Her father is the county surveyor."

"I have been invited to their home to dine," he informed us. "Could you tell me Audrey's favorite flower?"

"She has always indulged in the unusual and out-of-the ordinary. It is orchids, I believe," Lois explained unhesitatingly.

"A striking personality, a clever young woman," he added as if to himself. The conversation then turned to Carey, and Glyn was silent the rest of the journey. We had been invited for lunch to "Sunny Mount," and we both accepted, but Lois and I had duties in the Sunday School. We rushed off as soon as we were finished, leaving Glyn with Mrs. Stanford. When I returned home in the evening after the service, Glyn seemed in a talkative, pensive mood.

"I like the simplicity of that home, Ruth," he declared so spontaneously that he surprised me. He had been so cynical before. "The lovely luncheon was so deftly and beautifully served. You don't know how I recoil from the endless round of dinner parties and the sometimes senseless demands of etiquette. Tyrannical society has made so many claims upon me that I feel like a slave fleeing for refuge.

"We so often bow our respects to men and women we know only gain it because of wealth and not because of moral character," he went on. We laugh and talk like actors on a stage. Insincerity and hollowness mark so much of what goes on."

My cousin puzzled me. Sometimes he seemed so much the man of the world, yet at others, as one totally disillusioned and simple-hearted. Sometimes he spoke seriously and loftily; at other times so gaily. Was he diamond-testing or had he adopted some of the very veneer he detested in others?

"Mrs. Stanford's motherly manner towards me," Glyn proceeded to inform me, "drew me out to tell her things about my past life that I don't often speak about. She was in the middle of her story when we were there the other day so I asked her to continue it. Her detailed account enabled me to better understand the 'Sunny Mount' household and their viewpoint."

That you, too, might better understand Lois and the thread of the story as it is unraveled, it will be wise to continue her family history as told to Glyn and as I had known it, too. You remember that Mrs. Stanford had been deeply convicted. The following Sunday, she again entered the little Mission Hall; there she found relief from her sense of guilt and a completely new life began.

Why she was drawn back irresistibly to this humble group of believers, she could never explain except that it was God Who drew her. Sitting in her beautiful clothes and expensive jewelry, she listened intently to the message. To her understanding, there dawned the purpose of Calvary and its personal application to her sinful state. It seemed she could take in a measure of that awful suffering Christ had endured for all sin—for her sin! So completely did she loathe herself as she now saw her true condition, that she despised the deceitful outward covering that had draped such inward selfishness and "undoneness." Off came her jewels which she quietly deposited in her handbag. Her mind and soul were now completely absorbed with the amazing love of Jesus Christ to her.

Much of her past life seemed incongruous after such a look at Christ! Leaving the service, she returned home to search the Scriptures in her own bedroom. Taking an unused Bible from its box, she studied it for hours and through its words, concluded without doubt that she had been born again. Reading, on, she sought for the clue to Christian living and found help in the Sermon on the Mount. "Having food and raiment, let us therewith be content," she read. It was wonderful belonging to the family of God; it was great to suddenly realize that you were loved and cared for by a Heavenly Father Who knew all about your needs. So she sought to "seek first His Kingdom and His righteousness," and watch all the other things being added. How simplified life seemed that before had been so complicated!

The succeeding days saw her, in a very determined manner, go through all her possessions, discarding that which she thought was not consistent with being a member of the household of God. Cards, trashy books and music, beautiful cigarette holders, and wine glasses—all went from her life and her rooms. Some of her new dresses, too, were of no further use, and they were folded up and packed away.

Her parents were furious. Good church people, they felt their daughter's mind was disordered and special consultations were arranged with the doctor, and spiritual advisers. Varied treatment was ministered to her—entreaty, threats, indifference—but their daughter remained unmoved throughout. Her loving, unselfish, and thoughtful conduct in the home puzzled the parents. They feared that this happy life would become infectious and that their son, Edmund, who loved his sister dearly, would be influenced. Both were forbidden to attend any more services at the little hall.

Though missing the fellowship, Eleanor still clung to her Bible and the place of prayer. In the public functions, she would frequently embarrass the family by her Christian witness, and so the day came when she was told to pack up her religion or her suit case. Faced with this choice, she had no alternative—she would need to leave home. A legacy left her by her grandfather now came to her at the age of twenty-one, and made her independent. Sadly she left her beloved home and much loved parents to live in strange quarters.

At the little Mission Hall, Eleanor was welcomed and given some active work to do. Eventually, respect for the young preacher turned to true love. Their marriage, and later their going out to Africa, however, sealed her doom with her father. He disowned his daughter and forbade any further communications with the family, for her actions, he said, had outraged his ideas of decency and decorum.

Some eventful years were spent in Africa where the two children were born. Important translation work on the New Testament was cut short by the untimely death of Mr. Stanford. The responsibility of bringing up the children and providing for them had been placed upon frail shoulders, but she was conscious of God's assistance.

When Glyn had finished his narrative, he looked at me questioningly and said, "If what she calls being 'born again' happened to very many people there would be a revolution in society. Why is this type of Christian so rare? I mingle with many professed Christians who never speak of these things, and who live no differently from the rest of us."

With tears in my eyes, I exclaimed, "Oh, Glyn, that's just the tragedy of the whole religious situation. Such people do not live differently because there has been no inner spiritual change. They lack that divine inner luster that makes the human diamond sparkle. Ministers and other religious workers are often to blame because they do not preach about the awfulness of sin, repentance, and a new birth—a new creation received through faith in Jesus Christ."

CHAPTER THREE

A RIVAL

I was busy helping Jan bottle some of our garden produce. Glyn had been out on long rambling walks. He had climbed several of the mountains, poking around the little villages that lay nestled in the valleys. I felt our life here must have seemed uneventful to him for my extra time was largely taken up with work for the Church and the community.

Now it was time to get ready for the yearly Sunday School outing. Glyn was invited, but more or less out of courtesy, for I didn't think he would have any personal interest in this affair.

"You would have a chance to view another diamond you have not met as yet," I explained.

"You claim much for such a small community," he remarked. "Must be you were lucky when you staked claims at Bradleholme."

"It is unusual, I believe, but varied circumstances brought us together here. Such amazing providences surely must not have transpired without a master plan." Here our conversation was cut short.

Saturday morning the weather looked most unfavorable for an outing. It poured rain in a steady torrent until I could hear the rushing waters tumble down the hill and over the rocks at the back of "Mountain View," turning our little brook into a swollen stream, carrying grass clumps and branches with it. Fortunately, however, the weather cleared as we neared Bradleholme.

I smiled as I watched Glyn board the Sunday School bus which we had chartered, and thought of his Bentleys. He seemed quite at home as he sat with old Dr. Burns. Would Glyn detect this unusual gem? His snowy-white hair contrasted with the deep sun-tanned bronze of his prominent forehead. Although his gait betrayed his age, it was evident that eternal youth was in his soul and sparkled in his clear brown eyes. We would never be without Dr. Burns on a children's outing for he seemed to have a wealth of knowledge tucked away somewhere and never seemed to tire, making every minute count with a variety of surprise games, interesting as well as helpful.

As Dr. Burns left Glyn to lead some singing at the front of the bus, I slipped over into the empty seat. I watched the old man lustily enter into the children's choruses.

"He seems to enjoy himself," whispered Glyn. "I say, he is an intelligent old chap. What could induce him to come along on a bus run for country children and give them such a hearty piece of himself?"

"He's a most unusual man," I acknowledged. "He's a marriage bureau to the young; he's a law court for subjects disputed; he's a father to the orphan; he's a physician in illness and just the man for all kinds of emergencies."

"But whatever can be the motive?" Glyn queried.

"Christ's love in his heart, I would say. He's endeavoring to live out the Christ life. Many years ago Dr. Burns and his lovely wife and three children lived in Carlisle. A disease carried off all three children within a week. The experience grayed his hair prematurely, but instead of pining, he has made himself a foster-father to all children. I think he's endured the polisher's cruel disc and shines more lustrous as a result."

"How thought provoking!" Glyn said quietly. Was he contrasting his own bitterness with this man's cheery acceptance of sorrow? One never knew. "He's a grand master-of-ceremonies," continued Glyn, "and he could easily grace higher circles."

Now we were coming to our destination, and the conversation closed.

We had all been busily engaged for the greater part of the day. Races, games, refreshments, prizes—all had gone much as planned. Mr. Marchant, Roy, Sheina and the mothers set off on a treasure hunt with the children. Lois, Dr. Burns and I had found a comfortable seat on a large fallen tree in a lovely spot. Glyn and Audrey came sauntering up to our little group in time to hear me remark, "Dr. Burns, I do believe you've had a merry time today."

"Why shouldn't I? Could you expect me to be otherwise than happy? It really is 'more blessed to give than to receive.' We must show the world that it's true. In my younger days I would have hooted at the thought of happiness coming through entertaining a bunch of Sunday School youngsters."

"You've expressed just what I've been thinking," said Glyn. "I've been smiling numbers of times at what a certain London set of fellows would say if they had seen me running a three-legged race and actually enjoying myself. I would be ragged unmercifully."

I happened to glance at Lois. My combustible friend was ready—yes, had to speak.

"I have smiled to myself a number of times, too, Mr. Forster. My memory recalls a scene. It was when I was approaching Westminster Abbey, I noticed a ludicrous sight. It was a London set, Mr. Forster—a large number of fine, intelligent-looking young men wearing toppers and long cut-away coats. They all looked so ill-at-ease as they passed us on their way to some special banquet, given in honor of some charity."

"I can't see a thing to laugh at, Lois," Audrey retorted. "That is a very dignified part of our way of life. You haven't traveled in such circles, and so are ignorant of its demands." She gave Glyn a significant look and sat down on the traveling rug which he had spread out.

"I would like to hear more about this most interesting subject," Glyn affirmed as he seated himself on the rug beside Audrey.

"I think I can see what Lois is trying to get at. Carry on, Lois," Dr. Burns urged enthusiastically, as he nodded approvingly at Lois to continue.

"Many pat themselves on the shoulder and say that they are not slaves to some ancient and worn-out religious creed." Lois continued. "They say the Bible is out-dated, and we do not need to obey its commands, but those same persons are enslaved by some decree of fashion and conformity to worldly customs. One must needs be another 'pea in the pod' to have society's approval; let anyone dare vary the pattern, and he is immediately ostracized. That is fashion's liberty!" Lois insisted.

"In other words you think the eccentric a martyr," Audrey argued in well modulated voice, "and the multitude all wrong. 'In the multitude of counselors there is safety,' Lois." Audrey's seeming poise made me wish this woman would show her true self by losing her false self-composure, but she never did.

"I am not talking of eccentrics now, Audrey, but of liberty of action," Lois replied.

"But surely you are not classing all of mankind as cowards?" queried Glyn.

"Not all mankind—by any means. But what name would you give to the many who dare not consult comfort, or even personal taste? Apart from fashion, look at some other demands of popular opinion. A worshiper of Jesus is not refined if he shows emotion—either joy or sorrow—over such tremendous certainties as Calvary and Eternal Life. But we are uninformed and ignorant if we do not praise some popular actor or singer who does little else but act upon our emotions in some fictitious plot or scene. Thousands of intelligent men travel miles to see men kicking a ball towards a goal. The cheer they let out at Hampden is heard over a wide area, and is called a 'roar,' and no one thinks it emotional if a hat is waved or tossed into the air.

"It's no longer praiseworthy to have high ideals of constancy in courtship or marriage. The great mistake is to be 'square,' and so we can violate all rules of morality and sin hopelessly. If someone should break over on some bit of table etiquette, he is vulgar. Society countenances drink at dinner parties with all its attending repulsive after-effects!"

Audrey spoke now with cool sarcasm. "You're just out of things, Lois. You've spent formative years in Africa, away from civilization. Accept the *status quo* and fit in, rather than be the odd one out. Don't think you'll win out against prevailing currents. You take Christianity so seriously."

"I won't let the world squeeze me into its mold," Lois persisted. "There are those faithful ones yet who will dare to take the abuse that the world metes out to those who disdain its maxims. I count myself happy to be numbered among them."

"Come, come, Lois," Audrey argued, "you surely aren't arguing for us all to be after your pattern, are you? I do believe you would like to take us down your narrow lane of thought and impose your strait-laced ideas upon us. That's the worst of these pious ones—they've no give. I think it's a sign of greatness to be able to change." A wise man changes his mind—a fool never. "What do you think?" and Audrey turned to Glyn. "You've traveled in high circles abroad and at home. What is your verdict?"

"I am deeply interested in the subject Lois spoke of at the beginning—men's attire. I should like to hear why she thinks we wear top hats," and his eyes twinkled. "I withhold my verdict temporarily."

"Do you really want to know?" Lois asked. He nodded and she went on, "I was amused to read an article on men's attire only the other day. The tall crown, it said, was adopted by hunting gentry to act as a crash helmet if the horse threw them. But why they should be worn in a modern motor car on the way to a wedding, I can't say!"

"And perhaps you know how we came to wear the long-tailed dinner jacket, Lois," laughed Dr. Burns, greatly enjoying it all.

"Yes, that's as foolish a hold-over as the topper. The evening dress or coat of the gentleman was originally the formal attire of the country gentleman who always rode. The long coat worn many years ago became a proper nuisance while riding on horse-back, so our forebears had the good sense to cut away the front, tapering it towards the back, or cutting out a square from the front. But, we very intelligent people of the twentieth century still use this sort of 'old-fashioned' attire in going to public functions, when it was really the riding-habit of a country gentleman, riding to hounds."

"I declare, she's made us appear ridiculous," Glyn admitted. "Do you think we ought to lead a reform in evening dress?"

"No, Mr. Forster, by no means," Lois declared emphatically. "There are too many worthwhile enterprises to engage one's attention. I only cited these ancient customs of hundreds of years ago to show that those who sneer at a person for obeying Bible commands in doing a Christ-like bit of work are just as conformed to ancient rites, or more so, and to less purpose."

Glyn looked at Lois who had risen from her place on the log. "Bradleholme society must also try its tyrannical rule over the minds of others. No one would array such arguments who had not experienced the heavy pressure of the iron hand of conventionalism."

Audrey rose looking rather bored. "Here are the children coming. We've some organizing to do to get everything together."

So the group broke up and all gave a hand in the final preparations, and it was a tired but happy group of children who boarded the bus homeward bound.

I took my seat with very mixed feelings. One felt that intense emotions were bottled in the breasts of some of those who had taken part in the recent discussion. Lois's cheeks seemed a little flushed and her lips seemed to move occasionally in what must have been prayer. She was silent except when accosted by some young questioner. I thought I noticed a rather new expression on Glyn's face. Once or twice, I detected a slight twitching of the corners of his mouth as though his thoughts might be just a little amusing. Again I thought—but of course it was only a surmise—that he glanced once or twice in Lois's direction with a mingled look of perplexity and respect.

But something else I saw greatly disturbed me. Audrey and her "shadow" were conversing together almost continuously in low subdued tones. I was convinced as I saw the glances shot over their shoulders from time to time, that trouble was brewing—and that that trouble had something to do with my friends in general, and with Lois Stanford in particular.

*** *** * * * * * *

In the days that followed, Audrey's visits became more frequent. She seemed to find reasons to come on business several times each week to "Mountain View." It was astonishing how many local, necessitous cases seemed to demand our attention just at this time.

She was most curious about Glyn—his business, his plans, and his future movements. Through subtle ways, she usually obtained just the information she desired. There was only one Audrey!

I had been so busy that it wasn't until some days had elapsed before I suddenly awoke to the fact that I had seen nothing of Lois. She usually had managed to slip around several afternoons weekly. I now missed her visits and wondered if she could be ill, so Glyn took me around to "Sunny Mount." We found Lois just taking in her washing.

"Isn't there a wonderfully clean smell about clothes dried in the good open- air? One can't reproduce that perfume anywhere else," and she laughed as she took a snowy-white pillow case and pressed it to her face. How easy it was to please this young woman. At her own back door she found in simple things a joy that many another went abroad to capture.

"Won't you come in?" she begged. Glyn excused himself as he was on an errand to Glasham, so I was left alone with them. The fragrance of newly-picked sweet peas filled the little room.

"I've missed your cheery little visits. I came to find out if you'd been ill," I said, as I studied her face.

"Oh no, not ill, Ruth. It's a busy time of year, and then I know you've had so many visitors. I thought I'd save my calls for when things had quieted down a bit."

"Friendship needs feeding, Lois. Others cannot fill up the place that special friends have in our hearts. But how's your mother?"

"She has not been so well. Sometimes I am tempted to think our prayers for her are not being heard," she confessed. "Audrey was in yesterday and related cases she knew of persons who had had marvelous healings and who weren't half so religious."

Mrs. Stanford called me into her room and unburdened her heart. It was apparent Audrey's visit had disturbed this family. I was getting accustomed to the commotion that always followed in this woman's wake. Audrey thought she was stirring the little village out of it sleepiness, but her upheavals so often left broken hearts and troubled minds. Christ stirred whole districts, but His coming always meant mended hearts, freed captives, forgiven sinners, healed bodies, restored faith, and enlightened minds. I felt indignant as I thought of the influence this woman wielded in our district, and the religious guise under which she worked out her personal schemes. She was a sworn foe to real inner goodness. How long, how long would she continue?

Little by little I pieced together the trouble-maker's tactics. Audrey had hinted that Glyn Forster was her most devoted admirer by relating how bouquets of orchids had arrived at her door, prolonged games of afternoon tennis played, car runs and sight-seeing trips taken, and happy evenings spent at her home. All this had been passed on with a most over-bearing confidence.

"It is exhilarating to have a little breath of air come to our pokey village," she said. "We're all going rusty. We'll never win Glyn Forster or anyone else to Christ by being too religious. Our little church needs to introduce a skiffle group. Pious singing is all right, but these hymns belong to the Moody-Sankey era of a hundred years ago."

"Surely," Mrs. Stanford had replied, "we need to remember the youth of today, but the old, old story is as attractive to a dissatisfied soul now as ever. It is we Christians who need the zeal, compassion, and power so necessary to put it across. If Christ is real to us, we will be able to make Him live to others. What we need, Audrey, is more people truly born again."

Audrey had flushed, but immediately retorted, "Of course, of course; but we must 'be all things to all men.' We will have to drum up some new type of attractions."

"What would you suggest, Audrey?" Lois had interrupted.

"Well, prayer-meetings, for instance, are out-dated now."

"What?" the two had gasped in one breath.

"Why, yes, you can't drag young folks to prayer-meetings these days. They just won't attend. How about an evening at our home? We could all sit around in easy chairs, sipping lemonade while discussing problems of youth. How to date? When is a dance right and when wrong? How to dress? We could get some truth across in a more attractive setting.

"You ought to learn a little bit of modern slang, Lois. It'd spice up your prosy manner; we must talk their language. Glyn was only commenting the other day on how you talked so advanced for your youth; you seemed a bit old-fashioned to him. I told him you needed somebody to take you and shake you a bit. You are far too serious for exhibiting the freedom and joy of our religion. Shock Bradleholme a little and do something that would set old heads wondering and young heads talking: a bit of spice—a dash of pepper!

"I told Glyn that I thought you and your mother's ideas of religion were hindering the wheels of progress in Bradleholme. With your support, we could put this program across. Sheina and I are feeling a special burden on us to see this district shocked out of its apathy. We don't believe God intends us to spend an hour in prayer with Him when a short, peppy word will do. (Mrs. Stanford sought to say something but Audrey had insisted on continuing). Let's work up a football team; let's have tennis competitions. Let's get the prayer-meeting group out on a treasure hunt. Let's change our tactics on a Sunday evening and run religious films. Let's book popular speakers."

"And whom are you seeking to impress, Audrey?" Mrs. Stanford spoke quietly. "Surely we are not competing with the entertainment world. We have a goal, and a message, and our Master left us simple directions to follow. 'Follow Me, and I will make you fishers of men!' Prove to me through Scriptures that these methods were the ones adopted by our Lord and I shall be the first to approve. It was, however, the simple message preached in power that appealed to my heart. I was as worldly a young woman as one could find anywhere."

"You forget that's twenty or thirty years ago, Mrs. Stanford."

Mrs. Stanford's face had set as she spoke. "Audrey, your program shall not receive my support. Lois shall speak for herself."

"Lois will be governed by your dominant personality. Even a stranger like Glyn Forster can see that Lois has seeming strength only because of your influence. He believes, as I do, that Lois really should be flung out alone somewhere, like the rest of us have had to be, to test what are her own convictions and what are yours.

"Mrs. Stanford," Audrey had continued with a show of sympathy, "no doubt you've had a real experience with God at one time, but your sad life and illness have tended to shut you in from modern up-to-date life. Lois is young and untried. Glyn thinks of her at times as almost a child. He must see what is obvious to the rest of us, that her talk is meant to impress him."

Lois had risen from her chair. She saw that her mother had had all she could stand of excitement. Facing Audrey she said, "I have known you from school days, Audrey. I knew who it was that laughed at me before my unsaved school mates for reading my Bible. If I had not had my own dear mother's influence, you should have wrecked all my faith in mankind and in God by your studied duplicity. If mother, Ruth Aldersythe, and Dr. Burns had not pointed the way to Christ, the influence of your double life would have blotted out the beauties and attractiveness of the kingdom of Heaven from me. My mother's verdict is mine, and I am not intimidated by the accusation that I am her rubber stamp!"

This had brought the conversation to rather an abrupt ending and Audrey and Sheina had immediately risen, manifesting a confusion rather unusual for these otherwise over-confident young hopefuls.

"Mother cannot take any more today," Lois had said quietly but firmly. "We understand better how you truly feel now. We shall never cease to pray that God may open your eyes before you cause untold havoc. God be thanked it is at least out in the open."

Lois told me how troubled and disturbed she had been afterwards—not over her decision, but that her answer had been rather too tart for the charity required of a believer towards one who differed. She had gone to prayer, and her Scripture reading had been in Esther. "All the king's servants bowed . . . But Mordecai bowed not nor did him reverence." Lois had then turned to the New Testament and had read of Christ's inflexible will and His answers to the Pharisees. Only then had she obtained relief.

*** *** * * * * * *

Glyn's stay with me was beginning to draw to a close and I noticed that his step was lighter and his manner more buoyant. A rainy spell had set in which kept us confined. One wet morning I stepped into the library for a book and found Glyn with his papers spread out before him.

"Looks like real business, Glyn. This is quite a contrast to your leisurely manner."

"You have only viewed one side of me, Ruth," he said. "I deliberately put all business aside when I came here, but some correspondence needed attention so I took this rainy morning to get caught up."

"You've been a little difficult to understand of late, Glyn. When you first came you were bitter and resentful."

"Yes—and what am I now?" he asked.

"I didn't mean to disturb you," I apologized. "I just came in for a book. Answering that question would require quite an explanation."

"I wanted to speak to you about something in particular, too, Ruth. There's no time like now for me, if you can spare it." I sat down in the chair he indicated.

"But where am I now in my quest for diamonds? I was bitter and resentful about not discovering a rich find—but now, what?" he asked, watching me closely as he leaned back in father's large leather chair.

"You greatly puzzle me, Glyn. You are so very wise and demanding in your six tests of a diamond."

"Yes, and then I play false," he said, presupposing me.

"Well, it's hard to explain. You set such high ideals for human diamonds and then you appear blind to these same ideals when it suits your whims and fancies. You seem to fail to recognize them where they do exist and, in other cases, appear to admire those characters which manifest a total lack of those same qualities."

"You are meaning persons here in Bradleholme, particularly?" he questioned whimsically. "Not Audrey and Sheina by any chance?"

"Yes," I warned, "I think you are playing into the hands of Audrey, and she's taking advantage."

"Perhaps I am not playing, but very serious in my attentions to this woman of no small ability. As for her sparkling and dazzling qualities—they have won, I think, the admiration of no mean person—Dr. Burns. I notice Dick Marchant depends upon her considerably as well. Does not this new and original program she is initiating evidence that she is energetically working for the good of the neighborhood and is wide awake to its needs? I've been very diligently at work—though you think I've been leisurely—in my laboratory, studying human nature. My calls, personal attentions and conversations have been far from aimless. I think Bradleholme has its dose of green envy."

"You mean, then, Glyn, you have discovered no rare diamond qualities here in Bradleholme?"

"Oh, yes. I believe Dr. Burns is as genuine a diamond as you could find. And Mrs. Stanford has few equals," he said, "but there is some further laboratory work, under magnifying glass, necessary before valuating the more youthful ones. Some diamonds are under inspection for months before the diamond cutter can decide where and how to deliver a blow.

"I just popped over to see Mrs. Stanford yesterday and Lois cut me dead. Have my attentions to Audrey or Sheina filled your little friend with envy? The 'Kohinoor' was a gem of such unusual beauty that it was the cause of bitter strife. Now who is the 'Kohinoor of Bradleholme'?"

I hesitated a moment. Should I reveal to Glyn the double nature of Audrey and her recent ill-treatment of Lois? It would explain things, but a sudden thought made me shudder. Did I want to seriously direct the admiration of this ultra-worldly young cousin to Lois? If I did, would I be responsible for either an unequal yoking together, or if it did not result in this, for one or perhaps two broken hearts? No, I would leave Glyn to his own findings.

But at this point Glyn recalled my wayward thoughts by changing the subject.

"I understand through Dr. Burns," Glyn explained, "that Mrs. Stanford's case is not hopeless. He says that only recently a form of treatment has been discovered that in ninety-five cases out of a hundred promises most gratifying results. It is costly and it would need to be undertaken in London, under specialist care. I have asked Dr. Burns to obtain further information, but to keep my part in the investigations a secret.

"Ruth," he asked earnestly, "would you act as my agent in this matter? I do wish to do something worthwhile with my money and my life. You think at times I'm all froth, but Dr. Burns has inspired me with his example. When you told me of the Stanfords' difficult financial position, and of the independence of the three towards being objects of charity, I tried to think of a plan of aid that would add dignity to the whole affair. They must feel no obligation to the donor.

"Just how to disguise my offer I am not quite clear. The husband's work was worthy of remembrance, and it may be that a donation to the Society's funds would enable it to make a long overdue gesture of appreciation. Could you enquire of Mrs. Stanford the name of the society she labored under while in Africa?"

I assured him I would gladly do what little I could. A knock at the door broke up the conversation. As I worked, I mused on the many currents just now that were making our quiet Bradleholme a churning mass of turbulent waters. But some good would issue—of that I was certain.

But I must tell you a little about Glyn's history or you could never understand him and his present plans.

Glyn's great-grandfather, and mine, was a Forster from Northumberland. He had traced the family back to 1680 to a Sir Arthur Lawrence of "Ashleigh Lodge." The family had, however, lost its vast properties and great-grandfather was only a gentleman farmer.

Early in life, Glyn's father left Britain to go out to Africa, and he and two others staked some claims in the diamond fields around Johannesburg. Their claim happened to be rich, and so, of course, money flowed freely. He married a beautiful and wealthy young woman, Kathryn Glyn. Her mother was of Dutch descent, but her father could trace his forebears back to Wales and some interesting traditions wove themselves around the old name.

The marriage proved a rather loveless affair, for Kathryn Forster lived largely for show. A boy, Glyn, and a girl, Kathryn, were born to them, and an English nanny was procured. How fortunate it was for Glyn and Kathryn that such a woman shaped their minds in those formative years! A devout Christian, she read stories from the Bible; and as they grew older, endeavored to make them aspire to noble deeds by setting before them the examples of people such as Shaftesbury, Wilberforce, Bright, and Howard.

The mother looked upon it all as harmless nonsense. They would forget such ridiculous notions and she would guide them later. But nanny knew if she had the minds of these children until seven, she could inculcate Christian principles so firmly that nothing would uproot them.

How many times Glyn had wished to know his mother better. He would run to the window and watch the chauffeur open the car door for, as he thought, the most beautiful woman that ever lived. She seemed like a fairy princess in her flowing evening gowns. Then nanny would sometimes take the two by the hand and from a distance they would watch their most attractive mother flit here and there in a garden party.

His father would have been a loving husband and parent had he not been disappointed in love and unwillingly dragged into social engagements. He plunged into his business to forget, and as he grew older became stern, austere and preoccupied. Little time was spent with his son and daughter, who could have brightened his loveless marriage and made some returns to this lonely, though successful, business man. How little Mr. Forster knew the pleasure a romp, a game or a drive would have given his boy! Glyn did retain a few happy memories of times when he was permitted to accompany his father on his rounds at the mines. Mr. Forster wished his young son to follow in his footsteps and take over the business interests when he retired, so these contacts were red-letter days in Glyn's life.

Being a most affectionate child, he would fling his arms around nanny and cry for sheer loneliness. When baby Kathryn came, his joy was complete. He was four when she was born and he would stand quietly with her baby fingers twined in his, while she slept, for ever so long, just breathing in love. Kathryn was his very own sister. For four years more he took this baby sister into his lonely heart as a companion until he was sent to a fashionable boys' school. The less said of that the better, for here he came to know the meaning of sin. However, there were holidays, and nanny and Kathryn were the two people on earth he loved most dearly. Then nanny died when Glyn was twelve and he never got over the loss.

Kathryn was never too well, but she outgrew it and at eighteen seemed to give her father and mother great promise. She was sent to Britain to complete her education, for she wanted to be a doctor. While at Edinburgh she contracted polio and in a few days Kathryn's bright promise of a glorious future career was ended by death.

Glyn was heart-broken. The mother who had failed him in childhood could not help him now. She was proud of her son and doted on him. The love that had never given itself to husband and to children when small seemed to be idolatrous now. Everything he could wish for was lavished upon him, but her vision was so earth-born. She kept their beautiful home in a constant whirl of drawing-room parties and balls, but gave little time to cultivating the friendship and love of her own family.

Glyn, heir to a large, prosperous business, appeared unaffected by the interest he inspired and the popularity he enjoyed. He seemed full of spirits and always chivalrous, but when several years passed and he never became seriously interested in any of the season's debutantes, his mother began to take alarm. She became more open, at least to Glyn, in her efforts to fix his attentions seriously upon some favorable and eligible young woman. She made social engagements which her son was obliged to keep.

This became sickening and wearisome to Glyn and he revolted. He tired of their endless chatter. He despised their jealous intrigues as one sought to outwit her rival. The cigarette, flicked so skillfully from the long, well-manicured fingers, seemed out of place in the hands of a woman who should be his life-partner and the mother of his children. His disgust mounted when he watched beautiful women, the worse for a drink or two, lose all inhibitions and say and do the most unbecoming things. The eyes that looked blankly beyond him, the lips that tried to form words which would only come out in blurred and stuttering syllables, the hilarious loud laughter, the uneasy gait—all seemed so incongruous when he thought of the care these women had taken in choosing clothes and training in posture and good manners. All, all seemed to mock and repulse him. The phantoms of his ideals hovered about him; the ideals drawn by nanny so carefully before seven years of age had left deep impressions still. This surely could not be called "LIFE."

Glyn's decided ideas at first only piqued the mother. A trip abroad was planned during summer holiday to Italy and France and the Americas. As he neared twenty-four and only grew more rebellious, the mother dropped diplomacy for more determined methods.

One day after a conversation, Glyn, in a temper, walked out of the house and begged his father to let him handle some of the business in the London office and so escape from what to him was sheer torture. The father pleaded, but finally yielded only because there was nothing else to do. Glyn left home to better run his own life and choose his own friends, but it was not long before he found that again it was his money and position that interested people rather than himself. In a further disillusioned and unhappy state of mind he had come to me hoping for a quiet spot in which to decide what to do about it all.

CHAPTER FOUR

UNEXPECTED DEVELOPMENTS

We were seated at breakfast the next morning when a telegraph delivery boy rang our bell. Tremblingly the little yellow envelope was taken from his hand and handed to Glyn, to whom it was addressed. He hurriedly opened it and his face grew stern and white. Excusing himself, he went outside. I watched him from the window and saw that he climbed the steps to our lovely, quiet view. In Glyn's case, it was best never to ply him with curious questions. I knelt in prayer and, opening my Bible, read, "I will lead the blind by a way that they know not."

Glyn returned in about an hour. I had not heard him enter and my head was bowed over my open Bible. There was a subdued and chastened look about his countenance.

"I have been fighting out a battle and my better self has won," he volunteered as he sat down in a chair opposite. "Mother is seriously ill and father's cable asks me to fly home at once. She never approved of my move to Britain and she has a will like iron. Just as I had some interesting plans laid, mother's blocked them—or so I bitterly argued to myself. She has made herself ill over me before, but she is my mother. After all, a hurried plane trip is for the best. If she were seriously ill I could never forgive myself for neglect; on the other hand, if it is only her scheming to control my life, I shall soon fly back to prosecute my plans."

"You will discover that when God alters our plans, it is because He has better ones to offer us," I said as I rose to help make preparations for his immediate departure. While driving him to the station six miles away, he begged me to give more thought to the plans he had suggested the day before.

"Perhaps you can explain to Dr. Burns the reason for my sudden going. I am sure he will assist you," he suggested. "Try to expedite matters through the Society so that Mrs. Stanford receives the best medical help available, and additional financial aid. I would advise you to pay this check," and he handed me an envelope, "into your own personal account and keep my name out of it all. If any more expense is incurred, you know where to look. Write me at that address," he added, handing me his card with his African home address.

"Mrs. Stanford is the kind of person this world needs. To add length of life to such a woman is only a duty fulfilled to all mankind," he added firmly.

As we were hurrying towards the station platform, Mr. Cheedle saw us and loudly called, "God bless you," from across the street. Then rushing up to us, he shook hands so vigorously that mine ached for some time afterwards.

"I trust it's as a converted man you'll be leaving Bradleholme?" he questioned, addressing my cousin.

"I'm diverted just now, Mr. Cheedle, by an unusual set of circumstances," Glyn informed him. "I'm leaving on the next train due to go any minute, so it will take a little concerted action on all our parts if I'm not to revert to rudeness," and there was a twinkle in Glyn's eyes.

"Er, yes . . . yes, of course. Trust you have journeying mercies," and Mr. Cheedle quickly left us.

"Converted?" Glyn queried. "Whatever does the man mean?"

"The experience Mrs. Stanford has related to you is often termed 'conversion' and in some religious circles this theological term is used frequently," I explained.

"He could have been speaking Arabic for all I knew," Glyn responded. "Mrs. Stanford's experience was easily understood, but I declare that man is a puzzle. Let's get back to the plan we were discussing; you will do your best to put my good intentions into action?"

I assured him I would. He shook hands heartily and added, "Thanks for all your kindness, Ruth. You've helped me a lot—more than you'll ever know. I've staked some claims in Bradleholme. I'm rather keen to get back and continue my mining operations." He quickly turned and left me standing there. I watched his manly figure stride along the platform and disappear into the corridor of the train. I had really become attached to Glyn during these weeks, and it seemed as though a part of my little world had suddenly been sliced off and had disappeared as I waved him good-bye.

On my way home, I stopped my car outside "Sunny Mount," and entered. I felt the need of my friends just now. As I related the morning's events, I watched Lois's face for any expression of disappointment, but she seemed impenetrable.

*** *** * * * * * *

Glyn had been gone for two weeks and I had busily set to work on the plan he had left me to execute. Dr. Burns gave real assistance by getting into touch with the Society, which I learned from Mrs. Stanford was the African Bible Society. They acted quickly because of Dr. Burns' recommendations.

Lois came running in breathless a week later with a letter in her hand. "I couldn't wait, Ruth. I just had to come and show you what a wonderful thing has happened." Handing me the letter, she exclaimed breathlessly, "Read this for yourself." I took it, praying that no expression of mine might betray my knowledge of the whole affair. I read:

Mrs. E. Stanford,
"Sunny Mount,"
Bradleholme.

Dear Mrs. Stanford,

You will be surprised to hear from this Society after so long a silence. The excellent efforts of your husband in translation work have never been forgotten by us, and we are reaping the benefits in many ways. Being a faith mission, we did not always have the means at our disposal to remunerate those who so generously gave without stint of their lives.

We have just received a large donation which will enable us to repay a debt long overdue. Our Society has learned of your needs through a Dr. Burns and upon his recommendation we are able to offer the following:

1. This Society will undertake to pay all expenses incurred by you while under the care of Dr. Philip Reading, Harley Street Specialist.

2. Your small weekly pension will be increased.

The choice of Nursing Home, etc, will be left to your own discretion. We trust that you will accept this gesture as a token of our gratitude for the many years of sacrificial labor you and your husband rendered to this society. We are,

Yours gratefully,
THE AFRICAN BIBLE SOCIETY,
Edward Simeon, Secretary.
EBS/ms

"Well," I remarked, handing the letter to Lois, "that is a breath-taking surprise for you! How wonderful that at last your dear mother should have some real attention! I am sure your father would have wished for no better reward."

"We are all so happy," exclaimed Lois with great excitement. "Oh, Ruth, we shall need your assistance, and Dr. Burns's, too, in making arrangements. You will help us, won't you?"

During the next few days there was great excitement at "Sunny Mount." Neighbors were popping in to congratulate Mrs. Stanford. Lois was enthusiastic, and I could see that although never complaining, she had missed what Carey had always had—traveling and meeting people. Bradleholme friends meant much to her, but for the time being, she was girlish enough to think only of the suggested changes.

Dr. Burns had a surprise for Lois the next week in the shape of a job at a Girls' Christian Youth Hostel. Lois's eyes sparkled as she thought of the open door for which she had prayed. What she did not know was that Audrey had had a hand in it, for that young schemer had initiated the plan, being a personal friend of the matron, Miss Drake. Dr. Burns encouraged Lois in her new venture, believing that life among the young in a Christian atmosphere would be excellent. It was to be only a temporary appointment as the vacancy had been caused by illness and a forced holiday abroad.

I went with Lois to London to see her through an interview and to help her replenish a wardrobe for her new life. Glyn had written me reminding me that there was to be no stinting of money in supplying any need of the Stanfords which might arise as a result of the change.

With mixed feelings, we were ushered into Miss Drake's presence. She had an air of sophistication. Fortyish, she stood stiffly erect, a perfect specimen of a perfectly groomed woman. I sensed a little tenseness in the atmosphere as the two sized each other up, for women usually repel or attract one another within the first few moments.

Although faultlessly courteous, there was a lack of warmth for my young friend. Why had Audrey suggested this position?

As we returned to our little village, I could not shake off my uneasiness about the whole situation, but I could not pin down a tangible reason for my misgivings. Lois was joyous and expectant as she received a letter telling her of her acceptance to the post.

After farewells and partings were over, the village of Bradleholme seemed desolate. I watched the quiet hills, as the sun went down and thought of the never-changing God. How glad I was I knew Him personally and through the Scriptures. Lois had promised a brief day-by-day diary. She had said, "It's just to keep in touch, Ruth, and take away home-sickness. I don't want to burden mother with my problems."

With few letters from Glyn, those from London were the more welcome when they did come. Letters from Mrs. Stanford and Lois were in the same mail and after reading Mrs. Stanford's brief note, I eagerly opened Lois's. This was her diary letter:

Tuesday: Just picture me sitting by an open window in this big city—London. My feet are propped up on a little chair and the view opens out on a back-yard all enclosed. I don't know just yet how I shall like this new job. It is so very different from taking care of my dear mother in quiet Bradleholme.

These three-storey buildings used to be the better class homes of professional people, but today they are being turned into apartments, and so there are just the left-overs still visible of a one-time lovely district. Hawes Hostel has taken over three of these attached houses. We are fortunate to be very near a large shopping district. We aren't boxed in by houses on every side as the grounds at the back stretch quite a distance and so secure us some seclusion.

The lawns are mown and the grounds kept up after a fashion, but the minute care is missing; the lovely old-fashioned scented flowers, roses, and the well-kept vegetable garden are all lacking. A straggling rhododendron bush, trying its best to put forth a few leaves but looking old and decrepit, faces me at the center back. Quite a few of its companions straggle all along the fence. In between there are those laurel bushes which I always despised because their rapid growth pushes everything worthwhile out. In the middle of the lawn are a few odd trees that have tried their best to grow, but the soil looks impoverished. I wonder how my garden is growing. Are my pansies and nasturtiums coming on and still giving a riot of color? How I'd love just now to go and dig my nose deep in a rose, getting the touch of dew!

I've wandered—back to my job! I am to be the receptionist and to help with office records, etc. in the mornings. Miss Drake says my afternoons are largely my own, but I am to be on duty in the evenings.

Wednesday: Am settling into my job. A bit of filing done and a few letters written for Matron. Miss Drake seems quite friendly, but there is a feeling of frostiness in the air. Perhaps it is because of my inexperience. I will do my work thoroughly and give good measure running o'er. She has many qualities worth imitating.

Thursday: I am puzzled, Ruth. Are all these young people professing Christians? I couldn't tell by their dress, conversation or general conduct. When Matron asked me to take the fifteen-minute devotional period last thing tonight, I enquired, "Are these girls all born again Christians?" She turned her back and went over to her desk as she spoke, "Why, yes, of course, Miss Stanford. You didn't think they were heathens, did you? A healthier bunch of young Christian girls you couldn't find anywhere—and from the best of backgrounds." The phone rang and I left the room.

Friday: Nothing to report. Usual duties.

Saturday: In the afternoon I went to see mother. What a wonderful hour and how quickly it passed! Phew! I needed some strengthening, and I got it. I never knew one could feel so isolated in the midst of a crowd. Even among professing Christians, it seems unusual for a person to be a "separated" follower because of Bible standards. I asked mother about it all; did a Christian need to take seriously Bible commands about conduct or was everyone free to do just as he or she liked? She read me this from *Pilgrim's Progress*: (Bunyan gave three marks of a pilgrim's appearance).

First: "They were clothed with such kind of raiment as was diverse from the raiment of any that traded in that fair. The people, therefore, of the fair made a great gazing upon them; some said they were fools, some they were Bedlams; and some they were outlandish men."

Secondly: "Few could understand what they said, they naturally spoke the language of Canaan: but they that kept the fair were the men of this world; so that from one end of the fair to the other they seemed barbarians to each other."

Thirdly: "But that which did not a little amuse the merchandisers was, that these pilgrims set very light by all their wares; they cared not so much as to look upon them, and if they called on them to buy, they would put their fingers in their ears, and cry, 'Turn away mine eyes from beholding vanity,' and look upwards, signifying that their trade and traffic was in Heaven."

Dear old John Bunyan did not know he would help a young woman in the twentieth century keep her standards up and her vision clear. With such standards one wonders how the *Pilgrim's Progress* is still a best seller.

Oh, I must tell you about my visit to the Marchants' in the evening. Some of these good people are like signposts along the Christians' highway that tell them they are on the right road. Doubts and fear fly in their company. Mrs. Marchant is a refined woman with the marks of suffering visible on her countenance. Mr. Marchant is built just like Dick, only a much older version. He has gone bald but the graying bits of hair all around are curling up in spite of the barber's scissors. One would take him for an artist or a musician. His face in repose is rather grave, and then all of a sudden it lights up with a glorious smile which transforms the man. Pauline is my favorite. What a beautiful face she has! I would pick it out from a thousand. She drew me out to speak of lovely things. Funny how people can affect us by their presence: they impress upon us their conception of values. Around some, all I can think of is whether my nose is shiny, or my dress not properly pressed, or the seam up the back of my stockings not quite straight. With Pauline, I am impressed with the value of time, the golden opportunities open to us, and the greatness of God.

Sunday: Took a service here this p.m. and Matron was present. I talked on "The Birth of a Soul." Ruth, I did feel I should help the girls see that there should be a decided, moral change wrought by Christ in the soul.

My text was, "If any man be in Christ he is a new creature; old things have passed away, behold all things have become new." Afterwards there was a stillness. No one talked much as we waited around for the cup of tea. Matron broke into the silence by saying, "Come on, Judith, strike up a cheery note. We're all too dismal." In a few minutes there was a merry chatter, and the usual atmosphere was partially restored.

Sheila Wilding came and sat beside me. "I am interested," she volunteered, "in what you said. I do want to be a better Christian. You talked as if you knew Christ personally and your face fairly glowed.

Nothing happened to me when I decided for Christ, although I've stopped a lot of worldly things. I'm filled with fears and doubts. Matron says I should just believe. I try, but it seems a bit of psychology—think you are, and you are. Sometimes I feel fed-up and wish to finish with it all but I am spoiled for worldly pleasure and yet find no joy or peace in religion."

I looked up to see Matron eyeing me critically, but continued the conversation, "Jesus Christ's death on the cross brought a salvation big enough to satisfy a small human heart, Sheila. You've made a decision—excellent—but there's more to be done. That is only the human part, but God performs the miracle by giving us LIFE in our dead souls. We must be born again. "To as many as received him, to them gave he power to become the sons of God.' Receive Him and expect 'power' from Him to make you a child of His."

"Miss Stanford, would you help pass around these sandwiches?" Matron ordered.

Bother my blushing, but I could feel the red creeping up my neck and face as I thought of how I should have been more helpful. I was so happy about my talk with Sheila; I felt I was stepping on air. As I came to Judith, I stumbled over the upturned rug, and the plate of sandwiches went over the floor.

"Better on earth than in the seventh heaven," said Judith. "There are always thorns to humble us when our revelations are too lofty." The girls within hearing were laughing. Why was I so awkward? I did try to be more dutiful after that.

Monday: Matron has been harder for me to please. I haven't been able to satisfy her all day in the way I do things. She reproved me several times for being so occupied as not to be courteous. I apologized and tried ever so hard. Another visit with mother helped to right me. Glyn is back and has been to see her. An enormous bouquet of roses was there, and I knew they were his. Mother goes in for a serious operation soon. Ruth, help me pray it will be a success. Whatever would we do without her?

Lois's diary ended here. She is having a lively time, but "Mountain View" seems so lonely with those dear, dear friends of mine away. Memory has flooded my mind with scenes of years gone by and I have looked at Peter's picture again as a flood of loneliness swept over me. Lois is so much like him. I would do anything for that girl—so impetuous, so capable of indignation, so ready to love anyone handicapped or misunderstood. A second letter just received reminds me so much of Peter's letters. How I loved to read them—heart struggles just poured out, but I am giving way to self-pity and that will never do. Lois's letter is revealing and it is her life-story I am undertaking and not my own.

Dear Ruth:

How awfully good it is to sit down and write to you. I can just imagine myself in the cozy lounge at "Mountain View"—you in your lovely fireside chair, and I sitting on the floor at your feet. But my surroundings here bring me back with a shudder. As you know, some girls come here in the evenings to spend their time. It is a Christian home for girls away from home, studying for different professions, or working. There are handicraft classes; there is the library for students; there is the lounge for social gatherings. I am to make myself available for them all evening, and of course it gives me wonderful opportunities. But all is not a bed of roses.

Tonight I went out from the lounge into the library. On my return, I hesitated a moment before entering the slightly open door and so overheard what was not meant for my ears: "I say, isn't she a fright? One would think she had come out of the ark."

"Ah, but there is some subtle attraction about her just the same," someone interrupted in contradiction. "And she dresses tastefully."

"She's a religious crank, girls. I heard her telling someone that the way out of temptation was to take time alone in prayer with the Bible. Imagine talking that out-dated stuff to a modern miss of the twentieth century!"

"I like her face. I could take my troubles to her and feel she would understand," said another voice favorably.

"But she doesn't care how stuffy she looks. No make-up—one could not use her as a fashion plate to watch the changing styles. Too plain lazy—these religious folks."

"She doesn't need make-up. If I had her face, I wouldn't want to cover it up. And as for being lazy, we haven't had anyone so anxious to give us a hand, have we now? What about her visitation work among the poor?"

"Going religious, eh?"

I walked in with my shoulders erect. You know, Ruth, how hard it is for me to keep from attempting to set wrong things straight. I can't stand injustice. The girls were aware of the fact that I had heard some of their conversation, for their faces reddened considerably and you could have cut the atmosphere with a knife.

I suddenly became so conscious of my appearance. At Bradleholme, folks took us for what we were. Here, make-up, hair-style, and the cut of the dress are the deciding factors. I recognized one voice, that of Judith Armstrong. She is attending university here, but has done little studying since my coming, and I usually find her the center of attraction, in the lounge, nightly. She is extremely good-looking, and what a dresser! But enough for Judith.

I broke into the stillness. "You were discussing dress. As this is a Christian Girls' Club, may I suggest that we spend our mid-week devotional evening on the subject. Gather your information and let's thrash it out thoroughly."

The girls nodded an assent, and I felt sure we should have a warm but profitable discussion the next night.

Thursday: Last evening we had a hot time of it. I want to write you before it all grows cold for I know you like to know the mind of the modern-day youth. Pauline Marchant and Carey were delighted to join us. For preparation, I depended largely upon my Bible and the Holy Spirit's aid. As I entered the lounge, Judith looked confident. She sat on the studio couch surrounded by her admirers. She it was who led the way by saying she thought a Christian should win others by being as much like them as possible. "I find if I'm up on the latest hair-styles, dress fashions, films, etc., that I can get conversations started with non-Christians, for this is what really interests them. Now, what a ridiculous spectacle we become if we are too decidedly different. We want to make our religion attractive, don't we?" she questioned archly as she flourished her beautifully manicured hand.

"That's just the motive that should animate every Christian girl," I admitted. "A Christian is duty bound to tell the good news to others. Will her message be more readily received if she is marked as a Christian, or if she is so like the great throng that only in her message is she different? Any comments?"

"I believe a Christian should be the most attractive person out," piped up Carol, who sat next to Judith. "God made nature beautiful and bright—birds, flowers, and landscape. Surely He doesn't want His highest creation dowdy!"

"I know some professing Christians who are most unattractive in their appearance," Mary Arnot added. "Oh dear, they repulse me as I look at their drab clothes. Their thick stockings are usually twisted in rolls around their ankles."

"Yes, and their hair styles! Oh, I don't think I'd want to be a Christian in forty years if I'd have to look like that," Maureen volunteered.

"Carol has introduced an excellent argument," Pauline Marchant said cheerfully. "She declares rightly that God made nature beautiful and bright. Did you ever hold a lily in your hand and study it? Its perfect whiteness; its contrasting yellow; its stately stems with leaves so perfectly matched. Were you ever tempted to improve upon it with paint brush or scissors? Did you feel you could increase its loveliness by daubing it with some flaming color, or snipping out some new design on its beautifully shaped petals?

"Would you want to repaint the robin's breast or change his little, short, dumpy shape for that of the stream-lined swallow?" Pauline questioned as she glanced from face to face.

"You mean," Carol urged sarcastically, "we're to think of those people as lilies and robins? Oh, my, what faces and shapes! That takes a great stretch of imagination or a pair of fairy spectacles."

Paul steadfastly looked at Carol as she questioned further, "Did you ever cultivate what you call dull and drab-looking individuals? Some of them are the world's finest. Nature distributes her gifts fairly evenly. Fragrant flowers are not usually the showiest. The best songsters are often the more somber ones. And, though one might possess a beautiful face, an irritable temper or a miserly nature can in time mar the loveliest countenance, while an habitual kindliness of heart can lend loveliness to very plain features."

I couldn't keep still so I ventured, "Yes, we are not content with the variety God originally planned for the human family. There are no pale-faced lilies, and dainty forget-me-nots, or lovely demure violets. We all want the same flaming reds and pinks of the roses, and so we lose, in our desire for similarity, the essential loveliness and variety that should make the human family so very, very interesting. Nature is never boring, but humans cultivate such a sameness that men and women travel to the ends of the earth trying to get away from the general pattern."

"But," Judith moved uneasily as she spoke, "we are talking about the way we should look if our message is to be received. We aren't birds or flowers. We're terribly active, earnest, modern young women. Is it wrong to wear lipstick in order to be a more attractive witness?"

Sheila, who had previously spoken in my favor, burst out, "I never could think a Christian girl should use lip-stick. Our minister doesn't approve of it, and my mother would lose all her influence over me if she used it. I believe in being separate from the world."

I had not seen such animation the whole evening. Two girls at once pointed their fingers at Sheila, who had just spoken. "But Sheila Wilding, you perm your hair. Who's to decide what is worldly? What's the difference? One says this is wrong; another that. I can't see a bit of difference between perming the hair and using lipstick. Both are unnatural."

Judith looked across at Pat Laurenson. "You aren't a professing Christian. What do you think?"

"It's all rather silly—these arguments. I really expect a Christian girl to be different. Why should she imitate the world if she has something so much better—Eternal Life, as you say? Why should I exchange my place as an unbeliever if there is no difference?"

Nata, the nurse, had been quiet, taking it all in until now. But she sat on the edge of her chair as she spoke. "I wouldn't care how a person were dressed who rescued me from drowning, or took me from a burning building. If I were seriously ill, it wouldn't matter to me whether the surgeon or specialist had a long nose or a short one, if only he were skilled and had a love for humanity. It seems to me it all sums up to whether we really believe that a soul is worth the whole world, and that to save that soul is the most worthwhile objective in life. Religion is either a party and politics, or a life and death issue.

"And girls," she went on intensely in earnest, "Aren't we really acting hypocritically as if we were worried about witnessing for Christ, when we spend so much of our time on our personal appearance or pleasure? One evening of listening to the conversation in this lounge would convince an honest person of our need of revival.

"Be honest now! When you are looking in the mirror, what are your thoughts? Aren't they vain? Isn't it mostly how you can outwit a rival or impress some Prince Charming? I'll wager you seldom ever ask yourself as you make-up, 'Am I attractive as a soul-winner?'"

"Well asked, Nata," Sheila rejoined. "We know what prompts our primping."

"There are some sincere souls," I admitted, "who think the outward appearance has no connection with their message. One good chum of my mother's had a revealing experience. She was possessed with a longing to win others to Christ. One day an opportunity came for her to speak. She carefully prepared and prayed that someone might be led to Christ. While speaking, she noticed two girls who never seemed to lift their eyes from her. She pressed the urgency of her message with great fervor, and at the end invited all interested to remain behind. The two stayed, to her great delight, but instead of asking about the way of salvation they enquired about her curls! These had hid Jesus from them. Never again was her message spurned because of pride, for from that day she simplified her hair-style."

"One good man has said, 'We must watch that the modernism of our appearance will not nullify the fundamentalism of our message,'" Pauline interjected. "And yet, on the other hand, we want to give others the correct idea of the King we represent. We are King's daughters. Did you know the Bible speaks of a woman's cosmetics? It does in 1 Timothy 2:8-14. The Greek word for 'adorn' in this verse is 'kismeo,' from which we get the word cosmetics. Today our idea of the word embraces largely lipstick, powder, and rouge. But the Greek conception was an 'apt and harmonious arrangement,' 'order' or 'adornment.' The adjective means: 'well-arranged,' 'seemly,' 'modest.' If we are to portray the simplicity there is in Jesus, our outward cosmetics must reflect that. Our tidiness and cleanliness must reflect His purity, and our well-arranged dress should show the harmony and natural beauty there is in His Kingdom.

"Some Christians are slovenly and careless in their appearance. That is why many of you have received wrong impressions. That is equally wrong. I should study what colors blend well with my complexion, hair and eyes. If I am stout, I should avoid horizontal lines; if tall, I should avoid perpendicular ones. If my face is round, I should avoid center partings. This is the 'harmonious' and 'orderly' care that should be our objective rather than that of artificiality that prompts personal vanity which is so insulting to the Great Creator."

Carey had not said much, but she now quietly asked if she might not add briefly one thought. "I intend to go out as a foreign missionary," she informed them. "I shall be a foreigner and a stranger. My customs will be considerably different from those of the country in which I am staying for a time. The Bible likens Christians to aliens, strangers, and pilgrims. We often see Indian university students walking down our streets in their saris. They are unusual, but why should they adopt our customs when they are only here for so short a time?"

"Paul said he became 'all things to all men' that he might win them," Judith fired back. "Some most famous missionaries adopted native dress in order to win others."

"But they did not adopt the war paint, the opium pipe, the cannibalistic tendency, or the polygamous habits. They only became 'all things' in those things which were innocent and lawful," rejoined Carey.

No more comments seemed forthcoming, so I left them with one or two more thoughts given to me in prayer. "The subject of women's dress in the Bible is one concerning which little is said. Can any of you tell me how Queen Esther dressed? In the romantic book of Ruth, we are given no clue as to her dress habits. Colors, style, etc., are all omitted. Christ's mother and the other Marys are mentioned, but their clothes are not. We are told that a meek and quiet spirit is of great price in the sight of the Lord, which is just the opposite of dressing for attention. Read 1 Peter 3:3-4. The cosmetics of a Christian woman are to be the hidden qualities of soul. 'The King's daughter is all glorious *within.*' What time is squandered on the outward appearance; how little on soul culture—prayer and Bible study! Aren't we in danger of over-emphasizing the outward appearance?"

CHAPTER FIVE

GRINDING CIRCUMSTANCES

Another letter in diary form is at hand from my good young friend. It recounts the happenings of the week.

Dear Ruth: This is a rainy day, and a wretchedly cold wind is blowing. I can just see you writing away beside a cozy fire, and looking out now and again upon green hills and rugged, wind-blown pine trees. There isn't much to write about today.

Tuesday: We were all at the front, waving goodbye to a girl who was leaving for Canada. As her taxi drove off, a large car drew up. It was Glyn who got out, and I'm afraid I must have exhibited excitement, for Judith gave me a withering glance. Matron stepped up to meet him, and they disappeared inside the front door.

"I suppose you wanted a boy friend," exploded Judith as she glared at me. "I told you before that you were a 'square'—only a very good man would wish to marry you."

"That's the only kind of a man I should want," I replied, "and then only if it were in God's will."

"Don't act so 'pi'" she retorted sarcastically. "I saw you trying to get his attention. He travels in exclusive circles for I've met him at ever so many parties and house dances. How extraordinary your actions are. He'd never look twice at you!"

Just then Matron re-appeared in the doorway and motioned for me to come. "You mother's operation has been pushed a day ahead," she explained as we went inside. "Mr. Forster has kindly come for you. You're wanted at the hospital immediately."

I passed the bounds of good breeding by running upstairs two at a time, and quickly dressed in the three-piece outfit you bought me, Ruth. Glyn smiled reassuringly as he opened the door of the car. "But, my mother?" I questioned as we rounded the corner, "Is she in real danger?"

"No more than would be expected after such an intricate bit of surgery," he answered guardedly. "We thought it best for you to be near, but we have every reason to be hopeful, with so skilful a surgeon."

As the car sped along through the maze of London streets, I lapsed into silence. Forebodings sought to overtake a cheerful outlook, so I prayed earnestly. How I had missed Father! We had had to face so many of life's problems without a man's strength during the last five years! The manly presence beside me strengthened me. Upon arrival at the hospital, he insisted on remaining until danger was past. Ruth, he seems born to know when his presence is needed. He stayed at the bedside until we had had some reassuring word and then, when Carey and I were too engrossed to notice, he quietly took his departure. We didn't even thank him properly.

The stillness of a hospital ward, the nurse awaiting call like a ministering angel, a patient stirring now and again, the smell of anesthesia, the white drawn face of mother and the fight for life—all remain with me as I write.

Wednesday: Uneventful except for reports on mother's progress which are always "satisfactory" or "as well as can be expected."

Thursday: Visit to mother who is very, very weak, but gaining gradually. Glyn's floral gifts are beautiful; my little offering so small in comparison. Sister asked if this young man were a relation. His interest had been extraordinary.

Friday: Matron desired me to help get ready for a large gathering which takes place tomorrow night. A famous Christian worker, Mrs. Amery, is coming to speak. She has traveled in Australia and New Zealand, largely on behalf of young people's associations. Visitors are expected, and the girls are all abuzz. Our largest hall is to be used.

Sheila has been to see me and tells me her Bible studies have cleared away a great many doubts. She sees that the new birth is God's supernatural work done in her and to be received by simple faith. She encouraged me by saying that some of the girls would like to have another discussion.

Saturday: Matron unusually chummy and pleasant this morning. She seemed to praise my work. In the late afternoon she said she would like a chat in her office.

After some discussion regarding arrangements for the evening, she shifted to a more personal note: "You've such lovely, wavy hair, Lois. Couldn't we think of a better way to comb it for the big event tonight? We each want to look smart and put Hawes on the map.

"You see," she added, "you've been in the country with a sick mother. You've probably not been able to keep abreast with the times."

"Which way would you recommend, Matron?" I asked simply. "I am not a stickler for any one particular mode, providing I keep to my convictions."

"Cut it and perm it," she replied.

"But can't I find an attractive and becoming hair-style without copying the multitudes?"

"You think fashion all wrong, Lois? You don't believe in changing with the times? I gave you more credit than that, and I still believe you will find some of these notions belong to the legal Christian. We aren't under law but under grace."

"I would require a reason greater than the fact that some Parisian woman of purely worldly outlook dictated it. May I tell you my own experience and how I came by my convictions?"

Miss Drake nodded with a look, half-bored, half-cynical, and I went on: "I permed my hair at one time much against mother's wishes and argued for it in just the way others do. Standing before the mirror one day, I was deeply convicted of my wrong motives. I realized how ungrateful and discontented I had been. What if God were to meet me with my curlers and to ask me my reasons for wanting to be other than He created me? I would have had to admit it was a desire to be popular and look like others, personal vanity and, hardest of all to confess, a desire to be attractive to men. I could not face the challenging verse, 'Whatsoever ye do, do all to the glory of God' (1 Cor. 10:31). 'Whatsoever ye do in word or deed, do all in the name of the Lord Jesus, giving thanks to God and the Father by Him' (Col. 3:17). I begged God to cleanse my motives; He did, purifying my heart. Now I only want to please Jesus. You may laugh (for she had a smirk on her face) at my fancy but I was so deeply convicted that I could never put in another curler. No arguments for doing so have ever seemed weighty since then."

"If you can't perm it, then have a short cut. It's less trouble, and so attractive for a young thing like you," she proposed.

"I couldn't have a short cut either because of what the Bible says. That Book is to me what a Highway Code is to the motorist. It definitely states: 'If a woman have long hair it is a glory to her.'"

"But, Lois, surely you don't feel that our spiritual life depends upon so small a detail?"

"We may not forfeit salvation, but we could forfeit blessing and strength. If I desire to please someone, I study to know his preferences. Then too, I read that Mary's hair was long enough to wipe Jesus' feet, and that simple fact was important enough to be recorded in Scripture."

Miss Drake rose and looked at her watch. "We've already spent too long a time on this conversation, but I must say, Lois, that your hair is not your glory. How much older you look! You're not doing it by any chance to attract a much older man than yourself? I've known girls with freaky notions like that, and it accounted for their so-called convictions."

My face grew hot, but I answered quietly: "I know that to cut it or perm it could mean months of blighted inner joy and peace."

"Joy!" Miss Drake exclaimed. "You're no advertisement for joy. Your talks, while they seem to animate you, leave a depressing sense of conviction which isn't popular. I warn you, Lois, you'll lose your influence here. It's happening already. Your scope will be narrowed down to one or two eccentric characters but you'll never win the crowds."

I was silent, my fingers nervously rubbing the edge of the desk, but I rose to go. As we walked down the corridor she questioned me further. "I suppose you think that only those who come up to your rigid standards are Christians?"

"Not at all, Miss Drake. Many may not have had any light on this subject."

"You'll at least wear something in keeping for the occasion," she urged as we parted.

I would rather have gone to my room but I knew cook always appreciated an offer of help at these busy times. I slipped down and, while helping, all the past rushed before me: Audrey's taunts, Judith's contempt, the girls' whisperings, and now Miss Drake's subtle pressure.

Why the ever-present struggle? Not all Christians seemed to experience such opposition. Was I some strange, odd exception?

My eyes happened on a magazine lying open on the nearby table. There was an advert for "Katchem" Home Perm. It pictured a forlorn-looking girl before using it, watching enviously all the young men go for glamour girls. She stood alone as the males evaded her. But another picture showed her after using "Katchem." Now there was a line of admirers queued up for her. Underneath were the words of a famous film star (divorced three times): "I always used 'Katchem' Home Perm. Travel to stardom with 'Katchem.'"

What business did a trustful Christian girl have with such motives, Ruth? Mrs. MacRoberts, who had come up behind me, looked at me curiously. "Now, lookee 'ere, Miss Stanford," she said. "You aren't thinking of changing this lovely 'ead of wavy 'air for that!" and she patted my head and then pointed to the advert. "You just be your natural self. You'll catch your young man all right the way you are. They're all plain green with envy. We 'ear things 'ere in the kitchen. They don't think we can see through it all, but we've a keen sense of humor and we aren't exactly dunces even if we've never seen the inside of a university."

Sunday: Our big event last night went off great so far as numbers were concerned. Doubtless, too, truth was uttered. Twenty decisions were registered. Ruth, I cannot understand why the atmosphere after such a meeting should encourage talk about boy-friends, films, and dress, instead of a conviction for sin.

Mrs. Amery, a fine woman, fluently gave the Gospel message, backing it home with Scripture. There was no hint to professing Christians (and the audience was largely these) as to the cost of discipleship. When these young folks "decide" do they know what is involved in Christian living? Do they know that Christ must be Lord as well as Savior? Will anyone acquaint them with the after-demands of maintaining new life through prayer and Bible reading?

Judith seems to know all about me, for she told the girls I had the manners and dress of a stallholder in a country market, and that I had picked up some of my vulgarisms there. She says that explains why cook and the housemaids are so fond of me. How catty women can be!

P.S.—Glyn, who promised to see me again, has never turned up, and mother hasn't seen anything of him, although he sends fruit. Have you heard? I'm troubled about several things.

*** *** * * * * * *

Another week and another lovely letter from Lois. The events are best told in her own words.

Monday: Miss Drake has asked a converted film actress, Sharon Downley, to speak to us for three nights this week. She is to explain how young folks can make Christianity attractive to the masses.

Tuesday: I went last evening to hear Miss Downley speak. Her subject was: "The Christian Girl's Grooming." She said that we must be made-up if we would show the winsomeness of Christianity and would vie with the current attractions of today. Perhaps without meaning to, she laid open to ridicule all those who do not conform in outward appearance, to a pre-determined model. She showed such pity for the poor, out-dated, small-minded Christians who were in a straight-jacket because of a narrow creed which had been superseded by the superior twentieth century viewpoint.

Certainly she left no doubt in the minds of most present that a well made-up woman is a "must" if she is to influence the masses. She did not use Scriptures for her evidence on this point, but rather worldly logic and sarcasm. I suppose, Ruth, we are Puritans all over again in her estimation.

Wednesday: Another talk by Sharon Downley. This time it was on the need for adapting ourselves to the non-Christians in our modes of recreation. If the young folk will not come to church, we must meet them at the cinema, the golf club, the football game, etc. She advocated that the one who would gain others for Christ must be up on matters of style and must be acquainted with personalities in the movie industry and in the world of sports and politics. "Thousands will respond and make decisions for Christ," she said, "when they realize these prohibitions and legal attitudes, so prevalent a few years ago, are not religion, but only the whims and fancies of old fogies. We Christian actresses bring a wholesome atmosphere to the film industry and through our fellowship and prayer-meetings reach film stars whom the clergy never contact."

Sharon Downley is most attractive, and of course, a personality. Beautifully and expensively dressed, with make-up in moderation, she does make a picture. And the puzzling part, Ruth, is that doubtless there has been some change in her life, but I cannot see her standards written in the Bible.

Thursday: Sharon Downley again. She speaks for only one half-hour, but the discussions afterwards with open question-time are continued quite a while. I almost feel that the good that we thought we had accomplished here is being hopelessly undone. Both Judith and Carol certainly feel they have gained their point since Sharon has stated their case so clearly.

Ruth, I wish you were here. I do appreciate the visits to mother, and to the Marchants on Sundays. The loneliness and sense of isolation in a place like this at times almost makes me wonder if the minority can be right after all. I was really "down" all day today. It seems that the hunger some of these girls had, has been diminished. There is no standard whatever of Christian conduct. What can the few do against such a mighty throng? Sharon showed pictures of Christian film stars in strapless evening gowns to prove her point.

Saturday: I did not write yesterday. I was too confused and disheartened. But I stayed up last night with my open Bible in prayer. I just hugged the good old Bible afterwards. It washes away all the grime and soil we get when we have to mix with the world. How can I ever explain how wondrously clean I feel after a time alone in the light of eternal realities? Things seem to straighten out under the Bible's clear and plain teaching! Sharon's arguments faded into insignificance as I read the Sermon on the Mount: "And why take ye thought for raiment? If God so clothe the grass of the field . . . shall He not much more clothe you, O ye of little faith? Therefore take no thought, saying, 'Wherewithal shall we be clothed?' For after all these things do the Gentiles seek: for your heavenly Father knoweth that ye have need of all these things. But seek ye first the kingdom of God, and His righteousness; and all these things shall be added unto you." It seems we wise young Christians have transposed the order: look smart, pay a lot of attention to clothes, and thus seek the kingdom; Christ doesn't put raiment, etc., in the same class at all. He said Gentiles or worldly-minded persons sought these things.

The minority can win out. We can! We can! I have been too much on the defensive. I must take the offensive. I intend to labor more earnestly for souls. I intend to start a private Bible study group in my own room. I intend taking some of the girls over to the Marchants' on a Sunday. I see that an idle Christian is the only person that these questions can vex: others are too busy to ask questions about how to spend time on worldly amusements. If a world is lost, we must act as if it is. If a soul is precious, we must esteem it as such in our contacts. A young student in university who is bent on a goal does not care how idly the purposeless student spends his time, or advocates freedom. He or she studies to attain. So run I, that I may win a prize, too.

Sunday: A good time with the Marchants, and also some good talks with the girls—Nata and Sheila.

*** *** * * * * * *

Another diary-letter from Lois tells how she is fighting through and winning.

Monday: It's glorious to be alive to serve in such an age as this. How wonderful it would be to chat with you, but the next best outlet is this diary. I hope you can put up with it. Thanks for your own good letter. The reminder of diamond polishing was so helpful. Mother gave me several good clippings, and I'll share them with you. They did me so much good.

"There are little diamonds, or little bits of diamond dust, genuine indeed, but of no further use than to polish the larger diamonds. It is often very difficult to see why the strong, the bold, the uncompromising follower of Christ should be hampered and hindered by such associations, but they will be found at last to be God's most valuable purifying agencies, and we shall find them our greatest blessings. We are not to reject them, and try to get away from them."

"What a strange way to perfect a diamond—grinding it against another! But sometimes that very thing happens to us. Did you ever have to live with somebody with whom it was hard to get along? Or did you ever work with somebody that was just as irritable and unlovely as he could possibly be? Perhaps he was the other diamond, and God was trying to polish both of you by letting you rub together. Oh, don't fuss about it. Thank God for taking such pains to make you lovely and ask Him to make you just as Christ-like toward that other diamond as you can possibly be."

Isn't this advice good for me in my present set-up? I had forgotten though that the polisher mixes olive oil with the diamond dust when he polishes the facets on the surface. I think God has added some olive oil this week.

In the lounge this evening Evelyn Cross asked me for my secret for steady cheerfulness. She explained, "When we're all together we appear happy and jolly, but your joy seems like tones of a pipe organ—coming from deep within. We see you in the hall and there is a light in your face that doesn't need to be produced by the funny joke at someone else's expense."

"Speaking personally," Nata broke in, "my fun is rather like a rippling brook—water tumbling down shallowly over a few stones. Yours seems like the steady flow of a deep river. Everyone speaks about your shining face."

Judith eyed me contemptuously. "Anyone can produce a shiny nose," she objected. "Girls, you will only understand Lois if you know the motives that prompt her. She's out to catch a man much older than herself. She's out to get a lot of money." And turning to me she raced on relentlessly, "We know your financial standing. We know why you try to stand in well with certain relatives of a very prominent rich person. We're not blind or batty."

Tuesday: Dick called here with Carey and we all went out to the Marchants' together. Dick seems radiantly happy these days. Mother was feeling so much better that I was able to open my heart to her a bit this week.

Wednesday: Was out visiting with Pauline again this afternoon. My program of aggressive action is doing me good. If you knew just how hard your young friend is trying to be faithful these days, I am sure you would pray more for her. It takes great strength—strength beyond my own. I know where to find it.

Thursday: A day of pleasant surprise. Sheila Wilding came bouncing down the stairs tonight and burst into the lounge with her face aglow, and her eyes shining. "Oh, Lois," she exclaimed, "It's in here—new life, new joy and new peace. I can scarcely contain it. It was while I was reading my Bible that I came across that passage in 1 Peter 2:4—'To whom coming, as unto a living stone, disallowed indeed of men, but chosen of God, and precious. Ye *also* as *lively* stones, are built up. . . . He that believeth on him shall not be confounded.' I was just a stone before—dead, cold and inorganic. I believed and was not confounded because He is the living stone. He spoke life to me and now I'm a LIVELY STONE."

Judith turned on the piano seat and stopped playing, and the other girls stopped their talking and studying. "Let's sing something, Judith. Do you know, 'He lives, He lives'?" Sheila questioned eagerly.

As soon as the chorus ended, Nata interrupted, "Tell us more about it, Sheila. You make us envious."

"Well, it just has settled standing doubts. I signed a decision card in all sincerity, but nothing really happened to me. I listened to Lois talk about something that actually transpired—the new birth—but I didn't have anything that could answer to such an experience. I'm rather keen to tell my old dad. He's been worried about me since I decided for Christ. He says I'm not happy, and he's been begging me to go out and really enjoy myself. He won't have to say that now. My, I'm anxious to explain the difference!"

Miss Drake had come quietly into the room and stood listening. As Sheila finished, she said with great dignity, "Well, when you've quieted a bit after this emotional upset, we'll have a sing-song."

Nata, always rather outspoken, looked at Miss Drake and persisted, "Oh, it's a great change to get excited about religion. We're all so staid and so very proper. We can get ever so emotional about a date, or a new dress, or some piece of social gossip. It's a welcome whiff of fresh air blowing out the cobwebs of our theological thinking!"

Miss Drake showed little enthusiasm over Sheila's new-found joy, for she had more than once maintained that doubt was something you had to live with always.

Friday: In typing some extract from a book for matron today, a letter fell out. It was in Audrey's handwriting. Does she know Miss Drake, too? Why should she write?

Saturday: I came down the stairs this evening in time to see Glyn shutting the front door. He returned to his car, and Judith was waving him off. I wonder if I've done anything to hurt Glyn. He was so kind in the hospital and suggested taking Pauline and me to see an exhibition of jewels. What could have happened? It is unlike Glyn not to keep a promise.

I had the girls for a Bible study in my room. They do show an interest. Miss Drake has told me I'm not to speak any more about my slum calling. She says the girls have complained that such recitals of poverty, vice, and crime are too depressing. How unrealistic Christians (?) really are! It hardly seems possible that among His followers, so many shut their eyes to the terrible need about them!

Matron has also intimated that there would be a large Christmas party for Christian Youth and Staff, and that I would be expected to go.

Sunday: Nata asked if she could accompany me to the Marchants'. We walked through the park, seeing it was such a beautiful day. She suddenly startled me with her abrupt and frank question:

"Lois Stanford, how do you do it?"

"Do what?"

"Stand up to all the jibes and jeers you get for your individuality," she explained.

"In the first place, I don't stand it as well, perhaps, as you think," I informed her. "If you knew how weak I am in myself, you wouldn't admire me. More than once I've thought I'd have to give up the unequal struggle and leave this place."

"How did you carry on?" she queried as we walked on slowly.

"The Bible has been my life-saver, and Christ abiding in me has been my only strength. Each time I seemed about to go under, I've gone to the Scriptures for my support."

"But how do you get anything out of the Bible for our modern times? I can't make anything much of it," Nata questioned anxiously. "There's nothing about modern questions—no rock 'n roll, no dances, no theaters, no hair styles, no dating."

"It's not silent when you know how to study it. The Bible does lay down clearly defined general principles, and if we honestly desire to know the truth, we can apply these principles to any modern problem. The Old Testament abounds with characters acting out their life stories for our benefit. The history of the Judges and Kings is a plain recital of the defeats and victories of a nation cursed or blessed as they failed or endeavored to seek God's mind on their mode of conduct. When they imitated the nations round about, they fell before their enemies and became captives sore oppressed. When they cried to the Lord, and broke down the false gods and their altars, God heard and turned their captivity. Can't one find by close study a picture of our set-up today?

"Christ's Sermon on the Mount, Paul's instructions to his new churches, and Peter's Epistles and John's plain and implicit directions to young believers are a standard for Christians for all time and all ages."

"Will you teach me how to study the Bible, Lois?" Nata pleaded. And can you listen to a bit of ancient history?"

I nodded and she continued, "Well, I was brought up in an ultra-worldly home. My parents were both unbelievers. An aunt on my father's side was the only real Christian I knew. She sent me loads of tracts, talked to me, and gave me books to read. The tracts always helped to kindle our fires. I read only a page or two but flung it away. I tried again a few weeks later but I was bored stiff and stopped. But one night, in bed, I casually read a chapter; I read another on repentance, and that did the work. Dear me, how I perspired! In a flash, I saw myself as a sinner. I realized why Christ died for me on the cross. I jumped out of bed, knelt down, and there and then I knew God's great love had touched my cold heart. Everything was different."

There were large tears standing in Nata's eyes, as she stopped and opened her purse, looking for a handkerchief. "Excuse me; I'm being silly, I know. They say intelligent people don't show any emotion. I thought," she said, taking up the thread of her story, "that Christians would be glad. I told everybody, but many couldn't grasp the significance of the mighty change which had been wrought in my heart.

"But my worst trouble came from Christians in the hospital where I trained; Christians in the church, Christians in my social contacts. I could stand up to the mocking of the unsaved, but the arguments of so-called Christians stunned me. They thought I was taking religion too seriously. God meant young folks to have a good time, they said, and it was morbid and over-conscientious scruples that caused me to give up so entirely the world I had loved before. I was weak and gave in; my peace went; my first love vanished, and I've just been barely existing ever since.

"Your coming," she added, "has pricked me like goads. I've watched you in a Christian Hostel take cuts that I knew hurt you often."

Nata heaved a big sigh and looked wistfully into the distance. "Does my so called strait-laced religion repel you, Nata?" I asked anxiously. "Do not be afraid to answer plainly for I am a learner in God's school."

"No, indeed," she affirmed most decidedly. "It's most refreshing. We've watched you cheerfully do small duties not expected of you. You apologize when you step over newly scrubbed floors, and the household helpers adore you for it. Since you've come to Hawes, you've brought an alertness and zest we didn't experience before. When you enter a room, we feel a presence. You've got something we don't possess. I feel like a deserter giving herself up."

"If you've deserted, as you say you have, why not tell the Lord Jesus about it right here, and take up active soldierly duty from this moment?"

Together we bowed in prayer, having found a place quite cut off from passers-by.

"I feel like I've emerged into strong sunlight after having traveled too long through a dark tunnel," Nata confessed as we quickened our pace.

It was on our way back that Nata approached me on rather a personal subject. "Have you given Judith Armstrong instructions to pass on to that fine young man who has come for you twice? I could not but hear her tell him the other day that you had left word that you had other engagements so couldn't see him."

"I have never left instructions with Judith Armstrong. I came downstairs the other day, just as he was disappearing and watched him leave in his car."

"I may be mistaken," Nata informed me, "but I thought he looked terribly disappointed as he turned to go. Judith's a sly one. I'd watch her—and—Mary Gryson."

"I have all I can do to watch over my own actions," I answered, but her disclosures had explained some puzzling happenings to my mind.

They call us narrow-minded for being different and insisting on obeying convictions, whether the crowd does or not. Isn't it really the large bulk of professing Christians who are narrow-minded? They can't tolerate a minority standing by their convictions without keeping after them morning, noon and night. They aren't content until they force the few to become an echo. If they have the majority on their side already, why should they fear the influence of the few? It seems odd that they cannot leave us peculiar ones alone, if power really does lie with numbers and majorities.

CHAPTER SIX

GLYN'S GREAT OPPORTUNITY

On the same mail that brought Lois's letter came a short note from Glyn:

Dear Ruth;

Life for me is a mere jog trot these days. The diamond business is rather slow and dull at present. Not too many important finds either in father's business or in my own private research. The gem in the hospital, of course, has been tried and proved. Circumstances seem to have favored my scrutiny of the organizing genius from Bradleholme. The same forcefulness displayed in a rural setting is now bringing this clever personality to the inspection of the wider London circle.

I have been frustrated, however, in even getting a close up of your highly esteemed gem. Personally, I have been unable to catalog or calculate her. Does she shrink from a close contact with a diamond expert? I can find no other explanation for her studied avoidance of me. One wonders if "the big city" test has not revealed some "inclusion" or is she in the laboratory of some other diamond prospector? There is nothing like this business for producing rivalry and intrigue. Take good care of yourself till we meet.

Yours ever searching,

Glyn.

It was remarkable that Lois's diary letter should begin as it did. For my own part that sense of foreboding about Lois and Hawes has been rising towards a climax.

Dear Ruth:

Another Monday rolls along. Did you ever have a feeling of something dreadful about to happen? Well, that explains how I feel about things here at Hawes. Judith's actions continue to be most perplexing to me. I told mother about how she had given Glyn the wrong information. Mother feels that "time" orders all things in favor of truth, but when you are young it is difficult to wait for time. Mother thinks that if Glyn can't eventually see through Judith's character, he's not worthy of better friendships. Then, too, Glyn is not a Christian. You would be pleased to see how much improved mother is.

Tuesday: Sheila, bless her, is so bright. I saw her a little downcast and talked to her about not living on her feelings but walking momentarily by the faith of Him Who died and rose again. Because He lives—we live also. I tried, too, to tell her about the devices of Satan. These young converts have never been made aware of his existence and of the fact that he goes about seeking whom he may devour.

Wednesday: Dick and I were waiting at the trolley-bus stand. Carey had left her purse at mother's bedside so had to run back for it. We were so surprised to see a car draw up at the curbside. It was Glyn's, and he had it full. Audrey and Roy were there, but the others I did not know.

"Night out, Lois?" Audrey quizzed laughingly. "We'll be having another wedding one of these days, you wait and see."

Glyn looked at me and then said rather sharply, "So this is why you were engaged and couldn't go to the Diamond Display?" Then, seeing the dismay and surprise on my face, he said quickly, "How's your mother?"

"She's fine, but she misses your visits."

Audrey interrupted Glyn and prevented his saying anything further. "Things are exciting these days, Lois. I've a new post here in London. It's social work among the Africans and Indians who newly arrive in this country. It's most interesting trying to help them get settled into jobs, and breaking down racial barriers. Glyn has been helping me get started and has really been most generous with both time and money."

"It's a needy work," I responded, my voice sounding a long way off.

"Well, we'll be late," Audrey said commandingly as she looked at her watch. "Fifteen minutes to make it in."

As the car moved off, I felt a heavy weight at my heart. Audrey always seemed to get the breaks. My task at Hawes never appeared so dreary and monotonous as I for the moment compared it with the limitless possibilities and opportunities of Audrey's new position. Then, Ruth, I suddenly felt I should not be indulging such thoughts, but should rather rejoice in her success. Christ's enabling caused me to triumph.

Carey came up and I left Dick to explain our encounter. "Audrey Castleton seems created to dog your footsteps and trouble you, Lois," Carey said.

"But God gives the best to those who leave the choice to Him. See if it doesn't happen that way," Dick remarked.

Thursday: We had another discussion in the lounge. If the girls can ask questions and be led out to discuss what they think, it gives me more chance of saying a few words in season, than if I were preaching.

Nata began it. "Is there anything for the Christian beyond conversion?" she asked. "Sheila and I have been discussing that possibility."

"Religion again!" Judith gasped exasperatedly as she rose and strolled over to the window. "Can't we profess to be Christians without making this a convent? It's been nothing but religion, religion, religion of late."

"I remember Mr. McNight preaching on, 'I determined not to know anything among you, save Jesus Christ, and Him crucified,'" Sheila added, ignoring Judith's comment. "And I'm reading the Book of Acts. We've a long way to go before we make up the disparity between the Early Church and ourselves today."

"Oh, so we have some apostles here? Girls, meet St. Paul," Judith said haughtily as she looked around the circle for support.

But Nata was not to be so easily dampened in her enthusiasm. "No, in reality, girls, I want to do some work for Christ among hospital patients, nurses, etc. I find a terrible cowardice inside of me, and I'm hindered by thinking of how I appear to others. Can I expect to be altered?"

"Peter was that way before Pentecost," I answered. "But look at him later: he was emboldened to witness fearlessly, even at the risk of his life, because his heart had been purified by the coming and indwelling of the Holy Spirit. 'The blood of Jesus Christ cleanseth us from all sin.' 'Perfect love casteth out fear, for fear hath torments.'

"So many people seem to reach a dead-end. They act as if they've attained, when there is a continent of grace to explore and discover. Christians are like travelers. Some are just interested in saying, 'I've arrived.' They walk along the dock-side of a new country waiting for the return voyage home, bored to death; others leave the customs sheds and venture a few miles into the city; others take a bus, train, or private car and ride out one hundred miles or so. Then there are those who really wish to explore the length and breadth of that country; to them, every day holds some new fascination. To me, this is the way the life in Christ should be—daily explorations in the Word where we discover for ourselves the unsearchable riches of Christ."

"Have you ever traveled outside Great Britain?" Judith asked, anxious to divert the course of conversation.

"Why, yes. I lived much of my childhood out in Africa."

Carol laughed, and Mary Gryson giggled as Judith answered, "Well, that accounts for her stuffy ideas. Come, girls, let's talk about something else for a change. Who's your favorite television star?"

We had been politely dismissed. "We'll resume it again some evening," I told them as I walked towards the door.

A hand was laid on my shoulder and a voice in low tones questioned, "Has your Knight never found out yet that Judith is playing you false?"

"He's not my Knight, Nata. He's just been kind to mother, and his cousin is a very, very dear friend of ours." (You see, Ruth, what I think of you!)

"Well," Nata volunteered, as she studied my face, "The girls think the young medical missionary is the one you will fall for; I have a hunch differently, and I think Judith is for some reason working against you."

Friday: Several of the housemaids are ill, so I have had to give a hand with many household duties. Cook is so very kind to me that I like to take an occasional run down to the kitchen and chat.

Saturday: The Christmas celebration is so near. What about dress, Ruth? Any suggestions are in order. Glyn has sent more flowers to mother but has never been to see her.

Sunday: Matron asked me to speak to the girls again this Sunday as the other speaker could not come. I spent a good portion of the day in prayer and Bible study. I had read something about fasting and prayer bringing results, so wished to try the experiment in my prayer laboratory. Cook was so alarmed she sent to matron who was so unused to anyone thinking of going without a meal that she came to my room. "Are you sick?" she asked as she pushed her head round the door.

I assured her I was just trying out a Bible experiment. Why should such a thing be thought so strange, Ruth? It shows how far from being Bible Christians we really are in this twentieth century.

"Nonsense," Matron rejoined. "You're a youngster yet, and why carry the woes of the world on those young shoulders. You are much too serious."

"I do like the time alone before I speak for Christ. It is His message I want to give, and one needs to listen quietly and study."

"You are a decided, unusual piece! The girls seem either to love you or —"

"Hate me," I answered.

"Come on down and join them before the service, instead of isolating yourself. You'll never win them by moping up here. You've got to create an atmosphere."

"I'm with them so much of the time, Miss Drake," I pleaded to no avail.

"You've had long enough up here alone. Show yourself friendly."

I washed the tears from my eyes—yes, I had been crying, not for myself but for the great cause of Christ, so neglected, so little cared for. Upon entering the room I heard Judith gaily saying: "Only a few more weeks and we have the grand yearly event."

Mary Gryson tripped lightly across the room. "And what are you wearing?" she asked Judith.

"I've a dream of an evening dress, but it's a secret. Don't want anybody copying it."

Talk of dress, boy-friends, dates, and recent marriages occupied the time until Sheila spoke up and said, "Girls, can't we find an interesting topic of conversation apart from this small talk?"

But Judith was not to be easily diverted and as Matron entered, Judith archly asked me, "And what are you going to wear? I suppose you're too holy to wear evening gowns?"

"I'm not sure yet what I shall wear. I'm on special life-saving service, and I always consult my Superior."

"Lois shall have a beautiful gown for the occasion and she will show you all how tastefully a Christian can dress," Matron said authoritatively. She rose and announced a get-together in fifteen minutes.

Matron had just introduced me as speaker when there was quite a stir because an unexpected guest had arrived. It was Mrs. Melvern, president of the Girls' Youth Groups. She is one who, they told me later, loves to spring surprise visits at the different centers. It was good I didn't know who she was before I spoke. I liked her face and gentle, humble manner.

Prompted by Nata's questions regarding the after-life of a Christian, the subject I chose for my talk was, "Power for Service," my text being, "I beseech you therefore, brethren, by the mercies of God, that ye present your bodies a living sacrifice, holy, acceptable unto God, which is your reasonable service." Here I tried, Ruth, to show the need of giving over to the Holy Spirit every room in the house of our lives. At the new birth, the Holy Spirit comes to us as a guest, but (as He is likened to a dove) He never forces things but rather awaits our invitation. He convicts us of inner wrongs, and that is why we so often wish to keep secret rooms and locked cupboards from His gaze. When He is allowed, He will cleanse and fill every part of our being, using us to glorify Jesus. If He has all our talents, affection, and strength, He will utilize every bit of it in making the world see, through living sacrifices, the beauty and power of Jesus.

Mrs. Melvern talked to me for a few minutes afterwards. She is very troubled over the apparent shallowness of many new converts, and deplores the lack of spiritual hunger and willingness for sacrificial living.

On Saturday, I wrote a whole sheet to you about Dick and Carey's coming wedding but I must have mislaid the paper, for I cannot find it anywhere. I haven't time to rewrite it now, but when it turns up, will enclose it. Sorry.

When receiving the above letter, I did not think that I should so soon be in London myself. My father's sudden death has changed all my plans. What an autumn! Lois's mother has had a serious operation; Glyn has returned from Africa, never letting any of us know his plans; Dick has left Bradleholme for exams and final preparation for his trip abroad; and now my dear father has left us. What a shock it was to find upon taking up his breakfast one Thursday morning that dear father had "crossed the bar" while alone in his sleep!

Lois, Carey, Dick, and Glyn all came up from London for the funeral. I found Lois thinner and paler but there was something of a deeper spiritual quality which showed upon her countenance. What a blessing to have friends when one is sorrowing! Glyn was a little difficult to fathom. It may be he was unused to the thought of death, and not having the bright assurance of Eternal Life he could not understand our calm, even in the midst of bereavement.

It did not take a great deal of coaxing from Glyn to persuade me to come to his home. "Wren Glen" is my cousin's country home. His love for his sister Kathryn, had caused him to name it "Ryn's Glen" which eventually became "Wren Glen." It stood off the highway, nestled in a wooded glen, with the effects of a landscape gardener's skill apparent. It was not large, for he never intended it for purposes of entertaining, but merely as a hide-away from the encroaching social world. An elderly woman acted as house-keeper and cook, and her husband was gardener and maintenance man.

Modern contemporary furniture filled the low-ceilinged rooms, imitating old English homes of centuries ago; and although central heating had been installed, the open fireplace in his study specially indulged my cousin's love of meditating in front of a glowing fire in an unlighted room.

Accepting Glyn's invitation rather appealed to me because business connected with father's will demanded my seeing solicitors in London. And then I felt the loneliness here with "Sunny Mount" closed and now "Mountain View" robbed of the one occupant who had made life so lovely for me. The best way to forget a personal sorrow is to lose one's self in helping to carry another's burden. Lois needs me, I know, just now. Glyn and the others returned to London, and I followed some days later.

So it was that I was in the Metropolis where I could watch the storm clouds gathering round Lois and see her enduring the polishing of the Master Cutter.

Lois was not at all keen on attending such an event as this big Christmas celebration, but her position almost demanded her presence. Her mother, Pauline, and I all believed such an occasion could help to show Lois a phase of life which doubtless she had never had opportunity of viewing for herself. She entrusted the buying of a suitable dress to us, and we did purchase a garment in keeping with such an event but modest and becoming a Christian. When a letter arrived shortly after the big event had taken place, I tore open the envelope eagerly and read:

Dear Ruth:

Your kindness to me is beyond words. After all you have done for me, you will want a first-hand report of how this evening's affair has come off. I'm propped up in my bed with the bed lamp casting soft beams over my shoulders. Sleep was too far away, so I thought scribbling would help tire me, and while things are fresh I can write a better report.

Perhaps you know the Manvers. In case you don't, Mr. and Mrs. Manvers own a palatial residence and are noted for their hospitality. Being owners of large factories, they have plenty of wealth. They are professing Christians as well, and believe that almost anything we might call worldly is all right if done under a Christian's roof, and with Christian supervision. Hence, they have billiard tables, card parties, and dancing. This affair is a big yearly event held a few days before Christmas and is a great meeting-place for those interested in youth work. They have three daughters of their own.

Miss Drake had her old acquaintances to greet, but I was a comparative stranger. Unaccustomed to such an evening's entertainment, I was a little at a loss until I noticed some African medical students who seemed as ill-at-ease as I was. Making my way over to them, we were soon having a great time. My childhood days in sunny Africa where I had learned to love the carefree black people, were relived. How many times we had played together round their kraals! A number of Indian University students also joined us and we were really having some lively conversation. I had quite forgotten my environment and how out of place I had felt. I looked up to see Glyn watching me from across the room, and was taken by surprise for I did not know he was there. He walked off with someone whom I later learned was Gloria Manvers.

Mrs. Melvern and Mrs. Manvers joined our group for a short time. Mrs. Melvern introduced me to her companion as the helper at Hawes Youth Hostel. Mrs. Manvers soon excused herself as she made her way to one group after another. How graciously she filled her role as hostess! With what ease and what poise! But Mrs. Melvern questioned me a little as to my life and background. She told me my talk at Hawes had made her desire to speak further with me. She soon, however, left me to entertain some of her more important guests.

Looking all about me and catching bits of conversations, I could not help but think how much water runs over the falls to turn the wheel but once—if once! Such needless expenditure time, money, and conversation going into just one such evening's entertainment! It stunned me. Did I believe in a world lost without a Savior? Did I believe a soul was worth more than the whole world? Statistics had showed me that we were not making progress in approaching the goal of taking the Gospel to "all people." Had we, as Christians, no responsibility in fulfilling that last command, "Go!" and how could such obedience to Christ be consistent with spending time and money like this?

Looking across the room, my eyes fell on Judith Armstrong, beautifully dressed. She was speaking earnestly to Glyn and Gloria. Judith caught my eye gave me a withering glance, but Glyn never looked in my direction. He seemed absorbed in her conversation. The floor was cleared for dancing, and my heart misgave me. I felt, as a Christian, no inclination whatever to take part.

The band began to play and the dancers took the floor. Judith and Glyn were partners. I looked for a quiet spot to which to retire and found it in a window seat where heavy velvet curtains seemed to afford me some shelter at least. I was a stranger and a pilgrim, Ruth, and didn't feel at home in such an atmosphere.

I watched the dancers glide over the floor in that rhythmic motion so subtle and attractive to many young persons. I became wrapped deep in thought. What our elders would frown upon elsewhere, they condoned here. The dance was a place for free and unrestrained love-making set to music, and the partners could easily be tossed aside for an exchange at every dance. What envy, jealousy and strife this would naturally evoke! I wondered how popular the dance would be if the men danced with men and women with women. And why, if the dance were right, did the orchestra or dance band use the latest hits, the musical talent of ultra-worldly men and women solely bent on pleasure? Why didn't they think of dancing to a tune, the words of which exalted and glorified the Lord? If the main duty of man is to glorify God, why aren't dance tunes based on a religious theme?

The dancing in the Bible should be a safe guide. Miriam's dance among the maidens was a religious praise ceremony to celebrate a victory. I wonder how Miriam's dance music would go here! I had heard the argument that the prodigal son came home to a dance and not a prayer meeting. But doubtless the dancing in the father's house was a spontaneous expression of sheer joy and gratitude. The tunes used would be in keeping, and the words, if any, would also be on the same theme. The prodigal's past life of sinful pleasure had ended dismally in the swine pen without a friend in the world. It is impossible to imagine him jigging to one of the current popular tunes, so associated with that very same life of self-indulgence and sin he had chosen to leave behind. David, too, had danced before the Lord, but it was in joy because the presence of God, typified by the ark, was returning. It evidently wasn't too popular a dance, for his wife was horrified!

I saw so many pairs of young feet and thought to how little purpose was this great waste. Could the inspired writer say of these feet: "How beautiful upon the mountains are the feet of them that bring good tidings"? St. Paul had mentioned feet, too: "Having your feet shod with the preparation of the gospel of peace." My feet were not shod for such purposes as dancing. I had seen a Kingdom to labor for, and a Person to serve that demands my entire devotion. I am satisfied and happy in the certainty of my high calling in Christ! Tonight I was an observer and philosopher.

Glyn changed partners—I think it was Gloria Manvers next—and I saw the quiet, reserved young man acting a very different part this evening. How very, very far apart lay our viewpoints—he, brought up in this sort of atmosphere; and I, in a missionary setting with a quiet love of nature and books, and a passion for helping humanity! I didn't like the Glyn I saw, Ruth. It seemed he was a type of Dr. Jekyll and Mr. Hyde.

A young woman of some seventeen years came up to me and interrupted my reverie. "At last I've found you," she said. "Mother and Mrs. Melvern said I should meet you, Miss Stanford. They said you might put some serious notions into my foolish head, and I might help you to loosen up a bit. They think you have such advanced ideas and such serious ones for a young woman your age."

I studied her young face. It was beautiful, but one quite devoid of strength of character. "I'm Amyenne Manvers," she added. "And I want you to meet some of the young people at the next interval." She deftly arranged her evening gown and seated herself beside me.

"Have you danced, Miss Stanford?" she asked me.

"No," I replied, "I prefer to sit with my thoughts and strengthen my convictions."

"And what were your thoughts? They must have been pleasant ones," Amyenne commented.

"I was thinking how different my shoes are from those of the dancers," I laughingly answered.

Amyenne looked at my footwear. She saw the lovely pair you helped me choose, Ruth. She then turned over her own dainty but fragile high-heeled, silver, strapped slippers. "Well, yours are much more practical for walking and general use," she admitted, "but to what difference do you refer?"

"I have special shoes for special work. I am afraid I'm completely spoiled for any other kind. They are guaranteed to make the wearer happy, useful, and contented."

"You are interesting!" she interjected.

"You see," I went on, "I belong to a marvelous family, and everyone in it enlists for special service. I serve a King and am always on duty—always, everywhere! He gives me a complete set of clothes suitable for His commission and I was just thinking how my King would love to have every pair of those feet doing His service."

Amyenne studied my face. "I am trying to see what kind of make-up you use. I heard a group of men talking and they said they had never seen a bonnier and more expressive face. They're all wondering who you are! What do you do to deserve such compliments? I'm envious!"

"My King chooses my make-up—the oil of gladness," I replied.

"I do believe you can bewitch people," said Amyenne. "You've done so with Mrs. Melvern—so mother says, and to have Mrs. Melvern's good opinion is worth something. Now you're casting your spell over me. I must learn about the King's service to which you refer. But here comes my partner for the next dance."

I was introduced to several young men who asked for a dance, but I declined. Judith tripped lightly up to me and almost leered in my face. Touching my dress, she said, "You've gone part way—why stop there?"

"Part way?" I queried.

"Yes, you've come to a dance—quite out of keeping with your high profession. Think I don't know why? Some convictions they are, I must say! Just elastic enough to get your man and your position!"

"What do you mean?" I asked again.

"I saw you trying to make a big impression on Mrs. Melvern by talking to the foreign students. I wish I could act the part as well. New international headquarters are being opened at the New Year. Entirely new personnel are wanted. I never thought you so designing, Lois. Most of the Council is here tonight. It's great to have such a clever type of Christianity. It can suit two kinds of situations!

"But you're not adept enough," she went on. "You ought not to sit here by yourself and mope like this if you want either promotion or marriage. Nobody wants a wallflower. Seeing you are so helpless, I'll send someone to you." And she haughtily walked away.

Almost immediately a young man—the most debauched looking I had seen—came up to me. I shrank from him as he laughingly tried to pull me to my feet. I could smell the mingled odors of liquor and cigarette smoke as he leaned over to whisper something in my ear. I rose abruptly and made for the door opening out into the cooler corridors. Once there, I felt the cold air touching my hot face. I looked around me and heaved a sigh of relief. But I had not been long standing thus when a familiar voice reached my ear. "Lois, are you out here alone? Are you ill?"

I was relieved to see someone I knew, and poured out words of hot indignation at such impudence and ill-breeding as I had just witnessed. You know me, Ruth, when I am indignant. How I wished you had been there for me to speak to! But Glyn said rather warmly, "You are only meeting much that has repulsed me ever since childhood, Lois. Can you not pity me for being constantly exposed to such company? Do you wonder I sought refuge at Ruth's sanctuary? You are not enjoying yourself either?" he asked wistfully.

"I am not of this world, even as my Master was not of the world He moved in. I am conscious of being an alien among the crowd, but that only declares plainly that I seek another country. The servant is not above his Master. They hated Him; they will not be likely to understand me, His servant."

"You talk enigmas now," he answered. "But, you remember, I was talking before of diamonds. To be in your quiet home influence was surely no test to your diamond qualities. A diamond should be able to stand scrutiny and prove its truest worth. Do you remember one important quality—a diamond is hard enough to impress the hardest of surfaces and yet to be unimpressed itself? Has Lois, with all her past benefits, failed in her first involvement in scenes as she has just witnessed?"

The words of St. Paul flashed through my mind: "Endure hardness as a good soldier of Jesus Christ." It was a second challenge in a matter of minutes: first Glyn's and then this Scripture. I had not sought these circumstances, nor did I have any liking for them. I was only doing what I had thought was a duty in the post I was filling temporarily. There must be a purpose in my being here and some soul perhaps was present whom I should touch and impress. I would search for such a one.

"Thank you, Glyn," I said. "I have recovered sufficiently. I will go back. I will seek to leave my Master's imprint upon some life."

He smiled approvingly and led me back into the lighted room. Judith Armstrong must have been searching for Glyn, for she quickly spotted us and her eyes followed us all around the room.

"I think I know people you would like to see," Glyn said gently as he introduced me to the Cuirsons and left. Dear Ruth, how I wish I could talk face to face with you. The clock tells me I had better wind this up so as to be ready for the day ahead. I'll maybe get a chance to tell you about Mr. and Mrs. Cuirson when I see you in a few days' time.

***   ***   * * *   * * *

It was several evenings after the Christmas celebration that we sat together, Glyn and I, in the library. The conversation reverted to diamonds.

"How does my diamond shine?" I queried.

"Not very well if one goes by Judith Armstrong. She does not give a very glowing account of Lois at the Hawes Hostel. She deliberately tested her at the drawing room reception by sending Leonard McAllister to her. Jokingly she informed me as to how she had told Leonard that Lois was a religious prude unused to such gatherings. Between them they staged an act. I am afraid I did not hide from Judith my real indignation at such an unkind plot. I'm a diamond tester, you know, and I don't like to give away information before I have reached a final conclusion yet I was frightened when I saw Lois' face so white and drawn and thought of the cold of the outside air. I watched closely and followed her out into the corridors. I thought at first that your diamond had revealed a serious flaw."

"You had always said she would be truly tested when under the scrutiny of a diamond expert in the drawing room of a wealthy family. Providence has favored you, Glyn," I said, "and I should love to see Lois in a setting like that myself."

"I have an open-door welcome to Mr. and Mrs. Manvers' home, so come along with me this week-end. I'm rather a favorite with them—perhaps the fact that they have two unmarried daughters has once again afforded me this advantage."

I learned later that Mr. Cuirson, the famous violist, was to give a performance, and as Amyenne Manvers had taken such a fancy for Lois, she insisted on inviting her. It was to be a smaller and more select gathering than the previous one had been.

The night was cold and raw, but the warm, lighted room soon made us forget the weather. I seated myself near to Lois who was busily talking to Amyenne. Mr. Buxley, the editor of a widely read journal and writer of books, and Mr. and Mrs. Cuirson sat nearby, and we were engaging in conversation. Glyn, I noticed, was not far away but was partly hidden by the massive protruding wings of an ancient chair. Gloria Manvers, Judith Armstrong, and several smart young men were also within a few yards of the circle of which Lois was the center.

Looking at her sister, Amyenne said, "This is Lois, about whom I told you. She was going to explain to me her special commission. I believe you said you were in the service of a King?"

I could hear Judith Armstrong laughing sarcastically as she drew a little closer and said in a low voice, "This is really too good to miss!"

Lois flushed a little, but I saw her straightening her shoulders and drawing in a deep breath. I knew her well enough to know she was going to defend the cause loyally.

"I am an ambassadress," she replied sweetly. "I am sent on an errand of great importance, as I am representing a powerful Monarch Whose domains spread from pole to pole. I am on His 'Good News Publicity' campaign."

I could see Judith's beautiful face darken as she, in an aside to Gloria, spoke low, but loud enough for others to hear: "Monarch of pots and pans, vegetable stalls and scrub pails. She's on best of terms with the King's scullery maids and country bumpkins!"

Several laughed at the sarcasm, but I saw Mr. Cuirson rise and draw closer to the group. "I think I can explain that commission a little," and he looked around the knot of assembled individuals. "I'm in the same sort of service."

"What, Mr. Cuirson! You, a famous violinist, in the same service?" Amyenne questioned. Quite a few were listening now to the conversation.

"Yes, the very same. I happen to be a well-known violinist, but the King has many different kinds of people in His employ. Music was born in me, for when I could not read, I knew musical scores. God gave me that gift, so I don't deserve fame or thanks for it. Music is too sacred to be sold. The money I do earn, I do not hold as my own, but for the King. He has only entrusted it to me to use for the many, needy, hungry and homeless ones in His vast domain. We are just passing strangers in this country and are here on the King's urgent business.

"Miss Stanford," he continued, looking at Lois, "after talking to Ruth Aldersythe, I was able to trace your likeness to an old chum of mine. It is so striking I could believe I was speaking to the sister of Edmund Spencer-Morton, an old-time fellow violinist. How much I used to enjoy his company and your mother's sweet voice! I am told that you, too, have a lovely voice, and so may we explain our commission from the King of kings to our friends, in music? Do you know, 'On business for my King'? I usually sing and play it to explain to non-Christians my real business and thus seek to bear witness in each of my performances."

While he had been speaking, his wife had produced from his portfolio the words and music. Lois looked a little uneasy, but she soon gained poise as the music of the violin prelude filled the room. These hearts beat in unison and it was evident that the same motive controlled them. Lois's beautiful voice brought a stillness and hush which pervaded the room. I thought of what C. S. Lewis said about hellish, impish forces hating two things—silence and music. Then my mind was drawn to the words Louis had begun to sing:

"I am a stranger here within a foreign land,
My home is far away upon a golden strand;
Ambassador to be of realms beyond the sea,
I'm here on business for my King.

"This is the message that I bring,
A message angels fain would sing:
'O be ye reconciled!' Thus saith my Lord and King,
'O be ye reconciled to God!'"

Amyenne's face was lifted towards Lois, and there was a peculiarly softened expression written there. Glyn sat inscrutable as his long fingers played nervously around his mouth and chin. He was hiding some impression! Amyenne pleaded for another number, and so the entire drawing room group was lifted above much of the chit-chat that would usually have comprised the evening's talk.

When Lois had finished, we enjoyed Mr. Cuirson's violin numbers, his wife accompanying him on the piano. I watched Glyn rise and disappear with Gloria Manvers and Judith into the conservatory. I felt disgusted at this cousin, until it dawned upon me that he might possibly have method in his madness. Were these two tools in his laboratory for testing diamonds?

Afterwards, Mr. Buxley, the Cuirsons, Lois, myself and a few others gathered in a knot as we engaged in a discussion of the great racial question which was disturbing the nations. How good it was to listen to men like Mr. Buxley and Mr. Cuirson, for I felt I gained a great deal of sifted truth in a short time from these astute minds. But I was astonished to hear Lois able to quote from memory part of a quotation from Father Huddleston's book, *Not For Your Comfort.* I turned to see Glyn standing nearby taking it all in. Lois, for one so very young, was quoting intelligently several able writers' viewpoints on the subject. Her father having been in Africa, she had been brought up on just such discussions between other missionaries and her parents on this much mooted question.

As the gong sounded for dinner, Glyn conducted Lois into the lovely dining-room and for the remainder of the evening played the part of her attentive escort.

CHAPTER SEVEN

THE UNDERWATER TEST

Dear Ruth: Although you're in a suburb of London, you still are further away than I like. I'll just continue my diary as it brings you closer even to write. I'll fill in the many details when we meet.

Monday: This evening in the lounge, Judith Armstrong said she was extremely interested in studying one's character by observing one's hand-writing. She produced a book on the subject and then asked those of us who desired to know what the author said about our particular scrawl, to sign on a long sheet of paper. There was not much time to analyze the signatures but it was interesting. Quite a study!

Tuesday: Glyn had sent mother a beautiful basket of fruit which seemed too lovely to disturb. Its arrangement was perfect. Why does Glyn not explain to mother his failure to visit her? What have we done to annoy him?

Wednesday: I don't know whether or not I told you about the lovely new center a few streets away, which is being opened around the beginning of the year. Miss Drake is hoping for a promotion and transfer. The girls are all talking about her chances of receiving such as a reward for long and faithful services at this center—Hawes. This place is an antique compared to the modern furnishings and equipment of the new center. Such a promotion would surely be a feather in someone's cap.

Thursday: It seems foolish to write down the shocking events of today. You'll probably be seeing me shortly after reading this! I had gone into the little cubicle built off Matron's private office and was looking through files for data relating to the new center. The partition was flimsy and a section of the top was glass so that it might be lighted from the other room. The door had shut on me and clicked, locking me in when Miss Drake entered with someone else.

"Sit down, girls," I heard her say.

"We felt we just must have a talk with you," said a voice that I knew could only belong to one person—Audrey. I went hot and cold all over. I could not remain there and listen to a private conversation. I rustled papers and coughed, but the voice went on.

"I understand you're having loads of trouble with your new assistant and I thought I might be able to throw a little light on her case." I rapped violently and called, "Miss Drake, I am locked in this cubicle."

Miss Drake opened the door, but oh, how confused she seemed as she confronted me. "Why didn't you come out before?" she stammered.

"Because I couldn't," I replied. "As you opened the door to admit the guests the wind blew the door shut and it locked."

"Never let this happen again, Miss Stanford."

"I am sure I never shall," I agreed. "Is there something I can do for you while you are engaged here?"

"You may just stay while Judith produces some very, very serious evidence against you," she explained. "Then you may go!"

"Serious evidence?" I queried, almost staggering.

"Yes, Judith found this letter beside your book you were reading in the lounge. It had evidently slipped to the floor, but upon looking at it and seeing its nature she thought it ought to come to me."

"My letter?" I questioned. "What letter?"

"You needn't be so alarmed if you're not guilty, but your face is terribly white, Lois."

"Read the letter," and she turned and opened a drawer. "I had intended calling you in before the interview was over any way, so it's good you are here."

Imagine, Ruth, my shock as I held in my hand a sheet of the scented pink writing paper which mother had given me. The hand-writing, too, was surprisingly like my own, and the signature was a perfect forgery—for a forgery it most certainly was. It was addressed to Mrs. Melvern suggesting an interview at which I might disclose to her things going on at Hawes—low spiritual standards, etc., which would allow her to judge the suitability of Miss Drake for the post at the New International Youth Center. The whole letter was diabolically clever in that it mingled certain sentiments that were certainly mine hopelessly together with apparent motives, not to say methods, that could never be mine."

"Did you write that letter?" Miss Drake asked, as I folded the paper and handed it back to her.

"I did not!" I answered emphatically.

"Were you reading the life of Wilson Carlile in the library on Saturday?" she continued questioningly.

I thought a moment. "Yes, I was looking up something about the Church Army and its work of the past. I am in the library most every evening, but that does not prove me guilty."

"Well it makes the suspicion all fall that way. Appearances are all against you, Lois. Why not be honest? This letter is worded somewhat in your peculiar style, too, and the objections there stated I could easily believe to be consistent with your sentiments."

"I know nothing of the contents of that letter. Someone else has been doing deceitful work."

"None of the Hawes' girls would do anything like that! They've been here long enough for me to know their characters. Unless you had definite evidence against them, I could not believe it of one of them. Audrey, a personal friend of mine, tells me she confronted your obtuseness in Bradleholme, and that you were most awkward when she wished to promote spiritual interests. It seems you are not content to play second fiddle anywhere without downing the first player," Miss Drake affirmed with a degree of finality in her voice.

"Who did you say found this letter, Miss Drake?" I asked.

"Judith Armstrong, one of my most trusted girls. No suspicion rests upon her, I am sure, for she's a fine Christian, and her father's a very prominent member of the Council. Do you have anything to say to Lois, Judith?"

Judith moved uneasily in her chair, but looked at me as she said, "Perhaps Lois will remember that I told her she was acting strangely at the Christmas party. She made quite an impression talking to foreign guests and getting Mrs. Melvern's attention. Now I can understand what seemed unfathomable then. Lois needs a job. Hers would be finished here when Miss Petrie returned."

"I believe, Miss Drake," Audrey interrupted, "that Lois's actions can be interpreted more easily in the light of her over-strained conscience." And turning to me she continued, "The honorable thing is to own up here before this becomes public. We could hush it all up, but if it gets around—w-e-l-l-. You see, Judith's father is one of the trustees. The girls here whom you have helped would get to know, and there's your mother who is ill. And you would never want Glyn Forster to know, would you?"

"Audrey, I could never own up to something I have had no hand in whatever, not even to save face."

"You see," she spoke to me as if she pitied me, "if one has a jealous, proud nature under the guise of deep spirituality, one is very apt to have a fall. Good people have sometimes sinned most deeply! Remember, I know only too well how you obstructed the spiritual program in Bradleholme. You were a bit defiant, and now you have been humbled to make you a better woman. Anyone could see by the tone of the letter that the strain of spiritual arrogance runs through it all."

Audrey was speaking for the benefit of the other two, hoping to impress them. There was a tense silence and then I spoke, looking straight at Audrey. "I did not do it, Audrey." And then turning to Miss Drake, I said, "I have nothing more to add. Is my interview over? I should like to go to my room. I feel too stunned to be able to understand how such a despicable act as the one just mentioned should be attributed to me with no greater evidence than what you have brought forward."

Miss Drake rose haughtily, saying, "You may go. I shall see you later."

Oh, Ruth, how can I tell you the heartbreak! I was crestfallen. Audrey always triumphed. I threw myself on the bed too bewildered, too benumbed, to pray or think. My mind became the torture room for every kind of thought. Before I could thrust out one, another seemed to stand in its place. I, wearied with the contest, determined not to let self-pity or bitterness bide even for a short time.

I realized finally that the best counteraction was positive thinking. I opened my Bible to Psalm 73. David tells of the wicked prospering and he, too, was puzzled. "Until," as he says, "I went into the sanctuary of God. Then understood I their end." Continuing reading, I found another verse which helped me: "For promotion cometh not from the east nor from the west nor from the south, but God is the judge. He putteth down one and setteth up another."

My heart became strangely stilled, and a peace unutterable filled my soul. Ruth, I am horrified to think they would ever suspect me. I should never think of writing such a letter. God is the judge, and promotion or trial comes from His hand. Seeing I had several hours off duty, I slipped over to Marchants and confided my trouble to them. Upon arriving back at the hostel, I found a note from Matron saying I should come to her office on my return.

Poor soul, she looked as if she, too, had been through an ordeal, but she only asked me if I had anything to say to vindicate myself.

"Nothing, Miss Drake," I replied. "I am at peace and can bide God's time to clear me in this matter. If He chooses always to let the suspicion fall upon me, He will give grace to bear it. I am very sorry, Miss Drake, for the needless pain this has occasioned you."

"That is my own business, Miss Stanford. At times your impertinence drives me distracted. You've never approved of my methods, and you have repeatedly caused me to have misapprehensions about your future usefulness in this center. Your letter just verifies what before were misgivings. If you care to stay for another week you may do so, but if you prefer to go immediately, I shall not consider that you have left me without due notice.

"It will perhaps be best for us both if I leave immediately," I replied, "but do let me thank you for your many kindnesses and the valuable training on lines which my work with you has afforded me . . . ." But she was stiffly showing me to the door. I had only meant to show gratitude, but it seemed she took it for cheek. I was dismissed and went directly to my room. While I was packing, Nata knocked at my door. She had heard only vague rumors which I suppose Judith had started. I told her the bare facts. Nata sought out Sheila and we three knelt in prayer, committing everything into His hands. It was largely for them I felt. Just before leaving, I saw a piece of paper being slipped under the door. It read:

"We think you've had a raw deal. We don't believe you guilty of the things of which you are accused. We have a few clues and we'll work until we clear you, just you wait and see!

THE C.I.D. SQUAD,
Nata Rendall,
Sheila Wilding,
Evelyn Cross and
THE CHIEF, Mrs. MacRoberts, Cook."

P.S. I forgot to say, Ruth, I'm staying with Marchants. Will be seeing you later.

*** *** * * * * * *

After her dismissal at Hawes, Lois spent a day at "Wren Glen" with me. I could not persuade her to stay the night. She shrank from meeting Glyn. However, he came in earlier than usual and seemed surprised to see her.

"You're a busy person these days. You've no time for old friends. How did you manage a whole day at 'Wren Glen' when you've so many claims upon your precious time? Every time I called for you, you were either out, or going out or engaged to see someone else. London has altered you," he added, studying Lois.

"I don't know what you mean," she replied wearily. "I have been busy at my work at Hawes. Nothing else has claimed me much except mother and my slum visitation work with the Marchants." She was unusually reserved and unnaturally silent. Doubtless the thought weighed upon her mind that Audrey or Judith had informed Glyn of her dismissal and disgrace, and overspread with a cloud her natural high spirits. Glyn had an evening engagement, so left shortly afterwards. But better things were in store for Lois. The Master Polisher was not forgetting the proper admixture of olive oil which He invariably combines with the diamond dust for His grinding processes.

Of course, Glyn sensed all was not well, so I was obliged to tell him simply that Lois had had a frustrating and disappointing experience at Hawes. He looked at me quizzically, as if to draw me out further. "So providence has given me the opportunity to observe this supposed gem of yours in the 'under water test,' eh?" he questioned.

"Under water," I asked. "To what do you refer, Glyn?"

"One of the surest tests that can be put by a jeweler to a diamond is this water test. If there is any question as to its being genuine it is placed under water. There the genuine diamond sparkles and is distinctly visible. If a genuine stone is placed beside an imitation one there, the contrast will be most apparent to the least experienced eye. The glitter of the imitation is virtually extinguished."

"When thou passest through the waters, I will be with thee," I quoted almost spontaneously. "What do you think of Lois in the 'under water test'?"

"She sparkles there," he admitted. "But a diamond is practically useless except it has a setting, you know: a ring, a necklace, a brooch, a tiara, a scepter or a crown is a fitting place for a diamond. Some have been tossed about for years by ignorant natives who didn't know their value; others have been laid carelessly in a suitcase or drawer, the owners likewise unaware of their priceless worth. And others have been used for industrial purposes. Will Lois decide wisely regarding a proper setting?"

"I don't know Lois's future plans. She seems to be under water just now, as you were saying, Glyn. I suppose her next move is all unknown to even herself."

The next evening as we sat together, Glyn suddenly asked, "Is Lois going to seek another employment or will she be free to fit in with plans Dr. Burns and I were making for her mother? We think Mrs. Stanford needs a trip abroad to complete the cure, especially with the severe months of cold ahead. Lack of money being no hindrance, why could not Lois accompany her mother on a trip abroad for the next few months?"

Animatedly he continued, "She appears to be needing the change fully as much as the mother. Warmer climate and more congenial surroundings might give the lift physically and psychologically. At any rate, Mrs. Stanford's case necessitates one of her daughters traveling with her. Give them all they need for the trip abroad, Ruth, but remember the glove of the A.B.S. conceals the hand."

A few days after the above conversation had taken place, Glyn's mood seemed to change violently. He was sullen and irritable. He took it as a personal affront when Lois refused to stay with me for several days, and seemed touchy and sensitive whenever her name was brought up in conversation. If I commended her, he argued against it, and showed up some youthful weakness. If, on the other hand, I commented unfavorably on some immaturity of character, he would defend her like an advocate.

*** *** * * * * * *

Audrey Castleton rang one morning and made an appointment with me. I dreaded her visit, but had no lawful reason to refuse seeing her. What motive could prompt this visit, I wondered.

Snow flurries were seen through the window, and the winter wind blew in gusts. Our fire looked cheery and bright. Audrey breezed in, in quite a confident mood, well wrapped in a beautiful fur coat. As she drew near the fire, rubbing her hands, she exclaimed warmly, "It's grand to be with such good friends. Glyn was assuring me only the other day of my welcome here at any time. He has great plans afoot, and he's so exceedingly generous with his money where welfare work is concerned. He's consulted me about a number of projects lately."

"You've time now, Ruth, for a little chat?" she questioned as she noticed my lack of warmth. She drew her chair nearer the fire and sat down. "I've quite an important bit of news for you."

"I can always make time for important disclosures, but time never hangs heavy on my hands. I hope your news is really good news, Audrey."

"Well, I've been championing Lois's cause today. I've managed a private interview with Mrs. Melvern at her office and pled so earnestly that I believe Lois may get a new job as a result."

"Audrey," I gasped. "You've not made things worse by your interference, have you?"

"Worse!" she exclaimed emphatically. "How could things be worse than they are? She has been dismissed in utter disgrace. Lois has surely touched bottom as far as Hawes is concerned; she could not go much lower. Poor girl! I prophesied she'd find London difficult; she's so immature and inexperienced. You will remember Glyn and I were both of the same opinion in Bradleholme; we agreed that she would appear quite different when subjected to city influences and no longer tied to her mother's apron strings."

With that patronizing look that I so disliked, Audrey continued. "In spite of the way that independent child has treated me, I felt the Christ-like attitude would be to act the Good Samaritan to her in her sorry plight. She's truly been stripped of her good reputation and left lying unattended."

"I think the Good Samaritan has already made arrangements for Lois," I affirmed, but Audrey did not catch my meaning. "Have you quite played the game with Miss Drake in this recent move on Lois's behalf? I hope you have not placed her in a bad light with Mrs. Melvern."

"Oh, no! Miss Drake is my friend, but poor soul she's so stiff, starchy and dignified. She never gets down to the level of her girls. She could not possibly have had a chance at the new center! No, it was only my duty to appraise the situation to Mrs. Melvern, for she had thought quite a bit of Lois, even though the acquaintance was so brief. She would naturally wonder at the dismissal. I believe I killed two birds with one stone."

"But you were not one of the staff. Weren't you intruding? How did you manage an interview with Mrs. Melvern?" The questions poured out as I thought of how Audrey always had barged in and pushed her way into all kinds of situations.

"Well, you see, I wrote stating I had very important disclosures to make which could be of the greatest interest to the Council."

"But was the information yours to give, Audrey? You mean to say you got the interview on that basis?"

"I did, and succeeded. Mrs. Melvern was very chummy and took me out to luncheon afterwards, thanking me for my deep interest."

"Audrey, I am deeply troubled. You were a friend of Miss Drake. Have you wrongly represented her?"

"Bother Miss Drake! She can fight for herself. Lois should be cleared even if it is at her expense."

"You sided with Miss Drake and Judith against Lois, and almost crushed the girl. Now you come to me and appear her benefactress. You are still the same twisted, double character, and you leave a trail of troubled, sore hearts everywhere you go." I poured out these words in astonishment as I thought of the utter betrayal of first one and then another of her associates.

"Oh, you entirely mistook me. Lois is so inexperienced. I felt, to be perfectly frank, I needed to remind her in front of Miss Drake that she was not perfect. Surely you wouldn't blame me for that? You don't claim infallibility for Lois? She has been just a bit arrogant and sure of herself at times."

"I object to your insinuations about my very good friend," I said hotly. "Your attitude is so hard to reconcile with your past actions."

"Not at all! Not at all!" she interrupted me. "On the contrary, Ruth, I wonder that you did not step forward and champion your young friend. You have done nothing to see Lois's name cleared in this matter. I have always been fair and unbiased in my judgment of her—never unduly praising her, as you have done, and always conscious of her weaknesses. Can't you see that I've risked my reputation for her sake? If Glyn had thought so much of her, why did he not use his influence to straighten out this trouble?"

"How could Glyn know very much about this affair?" I questioned. "Did you tell him all about it?"

"I thought I would be fairer than Judith. He was bound to hear about it, as he has been a little friendlier of late with Judith than formerly. She could easily have placed a wrong construction upon such unfortunate circumstances," she explained suavely. "Glyn could become very prejudiced. I have had to put the best construction upon Lois's actions more than once to Glyn. You could have told him, I suppose, but then you would have only one side of the affair. I think it was another Good Samaritan act, really."

"You will not convince Lois you have acted on her behalf, Audrey, until you straighten out some past transactions. It is a precious thing to have another's confidence."

"Well, in spite of her continued dislike and refusal to make peace, I, at least, will endeavor to keep the unity of the Spirit even though she does not. If she thrusts aside my humble efforts, I shall not be to blame. I have done my best in getting her another job."

"Lois will not need it. A truly Good Samaritan got to Lois before you did, and she has been provided for," I divulged. "Lois and her mother are booked to sail on the 'Watonia' ten days from now and they will be abroad for several months. Amyenne Manvers is to accompany them. She will not need your assistance in the meantime, and much can happen to clear up the dirty work at Hawes in the interval."

"A trip abroad!" Audrey gasped. "It could look like she was running away from a bad situation."

"I'll get you a cup of tea, Audrey," I said, ignoring her remark. "You'll be going out into the cold and will need something. If you'll excuse me, I'll only be a few minutes."

Glyn had been in the library with his private papers, but he came in just as Audrey was preparing to go. "Did you succeed in seeing Mrs. Melvern?" he asked innocently.

"Yes," she said, as if anxious to close the subject. "I'll tell you all about it another time. I have a most important engagement in just half an hour. I am sorry to be so abrupt."

Glyn, with his usual courtesy, showed her out to her little car, and then returning, stood with his back to the fire, slowly shaking his head. "She still gets me doing things in spite of myself. On my recommendation she obtained an interview with Mrs. Melvern, and she seemed so close about it all. I've been drawn into quite a bit of red-tape lately through Audrey in behalf of the new center about to be opened. The expenditure of some money doesn't bother me, but she gets me into sticky situations which could complicate things."

"She told you of the affair at Hawes in detail. Remember, Glyn, there are two sides to every story."

"I am reserving judgment, but I cannot get Lois to tell the other side of the story. You saw how reticent she was with me the other day. She's treated me rather shabbily, and I can't understand why I've deserved such handling, especially without any explanation," he confessed.

"Perhaps she has no reason for believing you would care to hear her side of the story. She is not one to give her confidences lightly to one who had not proven beyond doubt his loyalty and friendship." A sudden ring of the telephone put a stop to our conversation for the evening.

CHAPTER EIGHT

BIDDING FOR THE DIAMOND!

Business obligations demanded Glyn's presence in Antwerp for some weeks, but he asked me to remain on at "Wren Glen." As he was to go almost immediately, I was free to give a hand with helping the Stanfords get away and still comply with Glyn's wish to keep his part in all the plans a secret. I accompanied them back to "Sunny Mount," and was absorbed in packing trunks and getting things in order for the months abroad.

One day, while busily engaged in final preparations for the trip, Lydia Scunthorpe dropped in. "Bradleholme isn't what it used to be with you all goin' to London like, and leavin' the likes of us to ourselves. And religion in Bradleholme isn't what it used to be either. Ah me! Ah me!" she sighed dolefully as she folded her hands resignedly upon her lap. Shaking her head most disconsolately, she continued, "We've squashes, daffodil teas, rose-arbor saunters, barbecues and hunts, but our little prayer meetin's aren't bein' attended. The sick are bein' neglected. Seems we're flowery like but not very practical. It's Lois, and yoursel' we're missin' mor'n that Miss Audrey. She had some queer ideas, so she did—I mean Miss Audrey."

"What do you mean, Lydia?" I questioned.

"Well, she'd no time for the likes of me and Mrs. Ainton. She aimed at bigger things and greater heights and forgot that it's little things we climb on—little rungs make the ladder; little steps make a journey; pennies make a fortune. Did she ever get that big job at the new place?"

"What new place?" Lois asked, dropping the garment she had been folding.

"Why that er' new buildin' for furiners from all parts of the world. I heard her sayin' to Dr. Burns that she thought she'd a good chance. She'd a special friend—Justice Armstrong—who could pull wires to get her in. Yu'd think she wuz a puppet what with havin' to have wires pulled," Lydia reported indignantly, "and she said Miss Lois had done sumthin' awful shockin' like and was in dreadful disgrace."

"Justice who, did you say, Lydia?" Lois queried.

"Well now, cum to think, I might be mistaken; maybe it was Armistice, but I thought it was Armstrong," Lydia explained as she tilted her head and looked down her glasses, giving Lois a thorough examination.

"You ain't so purt lookin,' Miss Lois, but you're better lookin' in spite of all the trouble, and sweeter, too, if you don't mind me sayin' so. I'm not one givin' over to flattery, but in my estimation there isn't anyone that can cum up to you. I don't believe anything Miss Audrey says, for she did me some bad turns onc't or twic't and covered it all up like. She ask't me to do something' fur her, and when it turned out wrong, she blamed me for it. She thought I wasn't clever enough to keep myself out of trouble. I told her I'd see'd through her all right. I'm not getting' fooled no more, says I to myself. Ah me! Ah me! Religion isn't what it onc't was."

And so Lydia had a cup of tea and left us a little wiser than we had been. Other friends dropped in one by one, and good-byes were said, but the cloud of suspicion still hung over Lois as she sailed out of Southampton harbor.

*** *** * * * * * *

A month or more after Lois' departure, Glyn returned from his business trip. He looked sad, dejected, and care-worn. He was silent and glum. February passed and towards the beginning of March, Glyn came to me one night about some business for the Stanfords. I read him parts of their interesting letters, but he seemed listless and disinterested. Not that he was less kind and courteous to me—no, he was kindlier.

We were sitting by the fireside when he suddenly let his paper drop and asked, "You won't go back to 'Mountain View,' Ruth, will you? You're the one homey influence that remains to me. I know I must be a boring companion these days, but it is a tonic just to know you are here. It's something like having Nanny nearby. I never seem to outgrow that childish affection.

"When's the big wedding coming off?" he went on without looking up as he pulled out his pocket handkerchief and opened it slowly. "I suppose I should be thinking of an appropriate gift."

"What wedding?" I questioned.

"Why THE wedding!" he exclaimed, with special accent on "the". "Dick Marchant's the man most to be envied in all the world."

"So you've heard about the secret. How did you get to know, Glyn?"

"One has a way of finding these things out. A diamond of such rare value is bound to have its bidders. I should have known Dick Marchant had all the qualities she would have wanted in a man."

"She? Whom are you meaning?" I questioned, suddenly becoming interested.

"Why, Lois Stanford, of course," he said almost savagely. "Nobody else really interests me."

"It is Carey who is to be Dick's bride," I informed him. I was going to say more, but Glyn suddenly rose and stood in front of me. He was violently agitated. My well-poised young cousin certainly was not himself.

"Are you really sure? Don't play with me, Ruth. I'm dead in earnest—never more so in all my life. I'm strong-willed and I know what I want. I've suffered enough suspense, but there must be something wrong. I have it from two other reliable sources," he contended as he again sat down.

"Then you have it all wrong," I explained. "It can't be reliable for it's untrue."

He studied me. "I hope you are right, but there are too many other circumstantial evidences which have to be straightened out. Take for example, the night I saw Lois and Dick together alone. I didn't bother visiting the hospital again; I didn't want to intrude myself upon the happy pair. Envious, I guess.

"Then there were the refusals to see me when I called at Hawes. I was built up on taking her to that Diamond exhibition. I had reasons for that trip, but she didn't even bother telling me herself. Then she wouldn't stay here with you but chose the Marchants'."

I explained the different circumstances which had appeared to substantiate the rumor of her engagement to Dick. As I told of how Judith had accused Lois of trying to attract him, and had given him the wrong information, his eyes flashed. "What must Lois have thought of my remissness!" he exploded. "Why didn't she let me know?"

"No really true woman is going to chase a man, Glyn, especially when she's been accused of such a motive."

As the floor lamp shone upon Glyn's eager, intent expression, I could see marks of suffering. This keenly sensitive young man of the world could not but betray the anxiety of the past weeks. "Well," he sighed, "if this is really true and I don't awake to find it a dream—then it is worth it all." His words finally convinced me that the real Glyn Forster was not as skeptical of my diamond as it had appeared, but had believed in Lois Stanford's worth from the day he saw her standing in the garden singing.

"I have been let down so often," he confided. "You don't know, Ruth, how utterly repulsed I have been by the mean, base motives that caused women to toy and play with my affections. I've always put a test that sooner or later revealed it was not really Glyn Forster but his money they were seeking. I have had to endure the constant attentions of false, weak and designing women just because I happen to be the son of a wealthy man.

"For the first time," he continued, "I have known a pure, true, and unselfish woman whom I could find it in my heart to truly love. She never flirted, either with myself or others; she had a mission, a goal and a purpose in life other than flitting about as a butterfly to attract the male of the species. Several times I used arguments to induce her to leave off duty toward her mother or her needy friends to satisfy some mere whim or fancy of mine, but to no avail. I grumbled inwardly but admired her for her steadfast purpose. One afternoon, Carey insisted on Lois relaxing and playing a game of tennis. I could see then that she had no strait-laced scruples about the game, but rather a more dominant sense of responsibility for the right use of her time and energies. I admired her code of values.

"She has always revealed some new facet of beauty upon closer acquaintance. Her talk was always purposeful, and uplifting. Most women's beauty and intelligence are displayed in the shop window, but Lois had the shelves of her mind and heart so well stocked that each time I window-shopped, I saw a most pleasing, varied display of both character and mind. Never have I come into her presence, but I wanted to be a better man. Always when she entered a room, she brought a fragrant influence."

He had been leaning forward as he eagerly spoke. As he finished, he sank back, his head resting on the back of the chair. I was deep in thought as I studied the leaping tongues of fire in the lovely grate, but was interrupted by a sigh which escaped Glyn. "Now that one fear has gone," he owned, "another has taken its place. Lois holds the key to my heart and happiness in one word. At least, she has not given her love to the likeliest man I know who could have had her simple one word—"yes"—bless his whole life."

"Tell me, Ruth," he pressed eagerly, "is there any other serious friendship? She could have met many likely and eligible young men at the Marchants'. I have told you how attached I became to Kathryn. When she died my heart was broken. My respect for Lois has deepened into love as I have closely examined her life and actions. Unconsciously it has grown upon me, and the rumor I heard, that she was Dick's, almost shattered me completely. Is there anyone else?"

How should I break gently to him the fact of her loyalty to the Lord Jesus Christ? I knew she would never disobey her Lord's command, "Be ye not unequally yoked together with unbelievers." Yes, there was a very serious rival.

"There is only one Other Who, I think, could possibly outrival you."

"Who is it, Ruth? Do I stand no chance in your estimation?"

"She gave herself to Another several years ago, completely, unreservedly and forever. Lois never does anything by halves."

He sank back wearily. "Is it anyone I know?"

"Glyn," I said, not wishing to prolong the suspense, "Lois is the possession of the Lord Jesus, heart, soul and body. He comes first in her affections. That has been her diamond secret—the Light of Life permitted to reflect and disperse His light through her life unhindered."

"Oh," he gasped. "I was more afraid of Dick Marchant as a rival. The other exists in one's fancy. If Lois has any regard for me, I'll soon override that difficulty."

"Oh, Glyn," I pleaded, "don't be too sure. You don't know Lois's loyalties as I do. Don't be too sure, Glyn," was all there was left to say to this determined young lover.

In the days that followed the conversation just mentioned, my cousin was as cheerful as he had before been glum. He suggested we drive to "Sunny Mount" and stay over the week-end. As I had been getting a book ready for the press, I was glad to escape the close confinement such work necessarily demanded. Glyn took along his gardener and the latter's wife, so it looked as if he wanted to make the moments count. We started early in the morning and Glyn was delightfully buoyant. Returning after performing a few duties at

"Mountain View," I found Glyn with notebook in hand carefully listing items for repair and for purchase.

Stooping over a clump of healthy daffodil buds about to burst into bloom, he touched one and said laughingly, "I've something in common with you—a bright, sunny spring lies ahead."

"Let's see," he mused, "they will be back around the middle of April. I've never had much incentive for gardening myself, but it shall be my own hands that tend this garden."

Sitting deep in thought as we drove back to London, I had very serious misgivings. Glyn must be prepared somehow for a probable disappointment. This young man, so bitterly disillusioned, and so much in need of the love of a good woman, was forgetting Christ and His claims upon his life. I shuddered as I thought of the fearful reaction which was likely to set in, if hopes were dashed. Here he was, building castles, without submitting the plans to the Master Architect. It couldn't help but fail. One day I had the opportunity I had sought.

"Glyn," I ventured rather timidly, "if you knew little of building and yet proceeded making plans for a very important edifice without consulting an architect, what would be the result?"

"Really, Ruth, the question is too childish to answer. I have been a man of business, and you ask a silly question like that. I wouldn't think of disregarding expert advice. I had the best of architects when building 'Wren Glen.'"

"But you are disregarding expert advice in your present building plans."

"How do you arrive at that conclusion?"

"You are contemplating building a home, and you are thinking of asking a little woman to give over to you her entire life-savings in character, love, chastity, and a promise of a career of her own, to help you in your proposed building. Have you submitted the plans to the Master Home Architect? The Bible says, 'Except the Lord build the house, they labor in vain that build it.'"

"Well, you do put things in a quaint way, Ruth. Surely marriage is between two people. I see no need to consult the Good Book on these questions. Religion has its place and helps one, but it doesn't poke its nose into all these private affairs."

"I'm afraid you do not know Lois Stanford with all your examinations. You cannot hope to win her consent, Glyn," I affirmed positively. "No matter how dearly she might love you, she would first consult His plan for her life. She believes that 'Whatsoever ye do, whether ye eat or drink, do all to the glory of God.' She has learned in small details as well as greater ones to, 'Commit thy way unto the Lord, trust also in Him, and He shall bring it to pass.'"

Glyn grew silent and the subject, of necessity, was dropped. Plans for their homecoming were eagerly discussed. His mind was as active for contriving pleasant surprises for them, but I believe my conversation did dampen his ardor somewhat, for he modified the proposed program considerably.

The following week, we revisited "Sunny Mount." Glyn was out early the next morning with his gardener and before the week was ended, numerous improvements had been made. A new gate took the place of the old one. The house had a fresh coat of paint; the roses were neatly pruned and tied into place along a new trellis. A garden seat with canopy stood in the shed ready to be put up a few days before their arrival.

As the day of arrival grew closer, he was more restless. He evidently felt he was nearing the end of his arduous quest. How many miles those long legs of his took him during this time of waiting I could never compute. This young woman he had at first appeared to disdain had surely and unconsciously captivated my formerly self-assured cousin.

*** *** * * * * * *

It was rather blustery, more like March than April, the morning the Stanfords' ship was due in dock. An eager, excited group met them and Glyn drove us all to his own home, where every possible thoughtful touch of preparation had been added. Glyn's household staff certainly caught the infection and did their best to give the very best impression possible to these guests who were friends of their employer.

Enormous bouquets of the Stanfords' favorite flowers brightened every corner of the drawing-room. Books, thoughtfully selected, were placed so as to catch the eye and interest the visitors. Glyn had always had an artistic taste, but now there was more heart and thought apparent in "Wren Glen's" appearance than at any previous time.

The visit was all too short to appreciate the many little detailed preparations. At best, travelers are anxious to reach the journey's end, and so Mrs. Stanford and Lois eagerly anticipated once again occupying their beloved "Sunny Mount." Glyn drove them up in his car. I had gone on ahead so as to have everything in final readiness. The passing of the last hour had seemed mercilessly slow as I listened for the sound of the approaching car. To help while away the waiting time, I had gone out to the garden where I sat reminiscing. My thoughts were miles away when a hand touched me gently on the shoulder. It was Mrs. Stanford. Glyn had stopped the car further down the road at Lois's request. She had wished to recapture her girlish feeling of exhilaration when approaching "Sunny Mount" on foot. She viewed the scene with all the wonderment of a child.

"My garden!" she exclaimed. "My, it is lovely! I pictured it all untidy. The gate! The house! The trellis! Look at the garden seat, mother," Lois exclaimed.

"The A.B.S again, I suppose," Mrs. Stanford suggested.

"They've studied our personal tastes then," Lois insisted. Then she threw back her head laughing. "Carey has been here. I had forgotten," she exclaimed. Wishing for affirmation of her statement, however, she glanced from one face to another for a clue to the secret. Glyn evaded the scrutiny by plucking up a tiny weed in the flower bed just at his feet.

Old friends dropped in during the next few days and the Stanfords, although having enjoyed their trip abroad, showed unfeigned appreciation for their own little home. They seemed to have brought spring with them, for the few days following were glorious ones. Glyn and I were preparing to go to Glasham to do a little business, so we stopped at Stanford's to see if we could combine it with a need of theirs.

"You promised Carey to see about that printing job," Mrs. Stanford reminded Lois. "It really should not be delayed another day."

Lois hurriedly dressed and in a short time we were driving along the winding road to Glasham. My business at the solicitors took me much longer than I had at first anticipated, and so I hurried back to the car. As I opened the door, I sensed I was coming at an inopportune time.

Lois was seated in the back seat, her parcels strung about her, and she was nervously stretching out the corners of her handkerchief—a bad habit of hers when she was a bit unstrung. Her face was flushed. Glyn had been half turning in his front seat, but conversation had ceased as I had approached. I had doubtless interrupted at an important juncture.

"I was longer than I thought," I apologized. "Am I intruding?"

"No," Glyn said. "You've known of my love for Lois, Ruth. I was just informing her of it."

"Well, why not drive out of this busy spot to our picnic grounds and finish your *tête*-à-*tête*. I'd love to take a walk round those parts again. You two can be alone and finish your talk. This busy thoroughfare is hardly the place to discuss and settle a question of such importance."

We drove to the spot I had suggested, but as Glyn brought the car to a stop and I opened the door to get out, he touched me on the shoulder saying, "Ruth, stay a few minutes and help Lois to see sense. I have excellent reasons, and lofty ones, too, for wanting her near me always. Her main objection is that I am not a Christian, but that only strengthens my point. Let me illustrate.

"Some years ago, I watched an expert dealer in gems looking over one of father's trays of diamonds. To the casual onlooker, all appeared similar, but the jewels varied tremendously in market value. It was of greatest importance that that dealer assessed each gem properly. How did he do it? He always wore a diamond of unusual value and brilliance on a ring on one of his fingers. I noticed that every now and again, he would transfer his eyes from the tray to the ring and gaze at it for some minutes. Then, he would again examine the tray before him.

"He explained to me that the diamond on his finger was one of the purest to be found. His eye would lose its sense of keen perception and judgment by so constantly studying jewels of varying degrees of brilliance and purity, but by repeatedly looking at the perfect gem he could return to his examination, thus safeguarding himself from making serious mistakes. Deterioration in determining price could not develop if constant reverting to the perfect gem was frequently employed.

"Now see the connection! I told you, Ruth, how skeptical I was when first we met in Bradleholme. I never thought then I would make such a find. Skepticism has vanished; faith in mankind has been re-established, and that victory should cause you and Lois satisfaction. Should I be reproached because upon discovering a rare gem, I desire to give it a proper setting? It is the only sane thing to do, but you raise objections to my worthiness—I am not a Christian.

"Ruth, do convince Lois that I am not an unbeliever in the highest sense of the word. You have witnessed my tenacious clinging to the ideals set before me in childhood. You know some of the scorn and ridicule heaped upon me for retaining those ideals in the middle of a materialistic age. I believe in God, but just because I am not 'born again' as you evangelicals term it, I am prohibited from claiming a lovely partner for life.

"The argument is downright silly. If the diamond expert needed the perfect gem at hand, so that by a glance he could correct faulty judgments in merely determining prices, am I asking too much when I ask Lois to be always at my side? The mistakes I can make mingling with humanity, ranging from good to downright wicked people, are far more serious than those of the dealer in gems. Why cannot I have her pure, good, noble and generous example ever with me to keep me straight? If she is always seeking to fill a need in this world, where could she find a greater one? My deficiencies and flaws of character ought to be my greatest argument for Lois becoming mine forever."

He paused and glanced at Lois. "Do you realize, Glyn," I pleaded, "that Lois has had no time to think this all out? You have gathered strength for this day for weeks, but you fling your arguments at her, taking her by complete surprise, and then you expect her answer to your questions which she could only safely give after time for thought and prayer."

"Does a buyer on the market for an exceedingly precious stone wish to give competitors time to gain the ascendancy over him?" he countered. "I tell you, Ruth, I know what I want. All these months I have studied Lois—she fulfills my ideals and I want her fiercely. Lois has it in her hands to turn me into a hard, bitter, cold, and calculating skeptic. She swings my fate by her decision," he affirmed passionately. He again turned to look at Lois whose eyes had been brimming with tears ready to tumble one after another down her cheeks. His look seemed to unleash those fountains as they flowed copiously and unbidden, one after another onto the brown paper parcel on her lap.

"Now, I've done it," Glyn said reproachfully. "I've always been violent in my decisions, but I have to leave for London in the morning. We were never alone for a minute. I had to take this opportunity and the whole world could have been going down that road and I wouldn't have been aware of it. I have been unfair in demanding an answer now. Take all the time you want, but do please remember that you have never in your life made such an important decision. The whole life happiness of another human being lies in your keeping. A lot hinges on one little word.

"Do forgive me," he continued apologetically. "What do you want to do?"

"Just time to think it all out by myself," she answered quietly. "Please, Ruth, could I come to your home. I don't want mother and Carey to see me just now."

"I'll take a look in at 'Sunny Mount' and say my goodbyes," Glyn suggested as he started the engine and drove along the road home. "I'll explain that you've stayed with Ruth for the evening."

Glyn's eyes followed Lois as she disappeared inside the door of my home and then he turned and said, "I'll walk over to 'Sunny Mount,' Ruth. I always love to walk when agitated. Don't bother with any dinner for me tonight. How could I eat when my fate is being settled? I'll be out until late."

He slowly walked down the drive, and I watched him out of sight. I thought of the night another young man had walked down that same drive after the same kind of an interview. Had my experience of the past been given to me to help my friends in this hour of temptation? I made my way into the house, and found Lois in her favorite position, kneeling on the floor. Her head was buried in her hands as she rested them on the seat of the old armchair. I slipped quietly out again, for she had not troubled to look up.

One hour later, I brought in a cup of tea and a few cakes. As she looked up, I could see her eyes were red and swollen, but the expression of agitation had gone, and peace had taken over.

"I must look a fright," she said. "I'll just run up and freshen my face with some cold water."

She came back down and drank her tea, but the cakes were left untouched. I heard strains of music coming from the room. I could not resist quietly entering the door, as she started one that she knew had been a favorite of mine:

"O Joy, that seekest me through pain,
　　I cannot close my heart to Thee;
I trace the rainbow through the rain,
And feel the promise is not vain,
　　That morn shall tearless be.

"O Cross, that liftest up my head,
　　I dare not ask to fly from Thee;
I lay in dust life's glory dead,
And from the ground, there blossoms red,
　　Life that shall endless be."

As the strains died away, she turned on the piano seat and said, "Ruth, let's go up above on the old stone wall. I know it's getting late, but we'll take the traveling rugs and pillows as we've done before. I want to talk to you."

We seated ourselves in this spot we both so loved. Leaning my head against the little whitewashed walls of the summer house, I watched the limbs of the tree above us move slightly in the gentle breeze. The light green buds were bursting forth. Spring was all around us but what was it bringing to my young friends?

"I want to show you something," Louis confessed finally, and opening her handbag she drew out an elegant jewel case. Handing it to me she asked, "What do you think of that for a beautiful diamond, Ruth?"

I touched the spring and a diamond necklace of most unusual beauty, embedded in a white satin cushion, sparkled and shone. "Oh, Lois," I exclaimed, "how exquisite! How it disperses light—and look at the many, many facets!"

She watched me as I studied it. "It is beautiful, but the story which accompanies it is even more so. It was Kathryn's. She had been given this unusual pink diamond of rare worth just prior to her sailing to Britain to study medicine. When she became ill, she had asked for a solicitor, placed it in his hands before witnesses and had requested that, in the event of her death, this priceless bit of jewelry should become Glyn's. She stipulated further that it should eventually belong to the woman who, in Glyn's estimation, could make him happier than she had done."

I gazed, and studied the diamond as Lois talked, turning it at different angles and catching the varied hues and colors it so amazingly shone forth. "It makes this diamond lovelier than ever. It has a history," I said softly.

Lois sighed deeply as she rose and readjusted the rug, drawing it closer around her, and turning towards me, continued: "Glyn handed me this jewel case at the beginning of our talk together and first explained about his sister Kathryn. Of course, I was deeply moved. Then he told me the same story he told you about the diamond expert needing the true gem to help him detect the faulty ones. He has used that argument in asking me to become his life-partner. But you've heard his arguments. I don't need to go into them. His offer has been a tempting one, because my own feelings for him are deeper than those of a mere friend. I had never allowed myself time to analyze his reaction to me. Audrey and Judith so ridiculed the idea of such a preposterous notion, that I completely thrust it from me when it would intrude upon my thoughts. After all, it did seem fantastic that a man of the world should ever think seriously of such a simpleton as myself. Of course, too, there was this insuperable barrier—he was not a Christian.

"Oh, Ruth, the difficult part is that my decision involves hurting him. I could stand to sacrifice and suffer myself. I have made repeated decisions that were costly. I wanted further education, but dear mother came first. I never, never regretted that decision. This, however, is so different. Glyn has had so little love and understanding, and he was so hopeful of my returning to him what he had missed. I wish he had never spoken it all out to me. My loyalties to Jesus Christ have been severely tested, and his arguments are subtle. God must give me strength to stand by Bible convictions in the face of the fiercest temptation that has ever come to me—the love of a man like Glyn Forster."

"Diamond testing," I reminded Lois. "Glyn thinks he has finished testing his gem, but God saw there was a bit of severe testing to be done to prove its purity. Glyn Forster does not believe that the love of a soul for Christ is stronger than the love of a woman for a man."

"Lois, perhaps I 'came to the kingdom' for such a time as this. It was to this same spot that I came to fight out my battle when your Uncle Peter had left me to make a similar decision. I loved Peter, but he was not a believer. I know your heart-break, for I passed through the same experience. One never regrets a choice when Christ is put first and foremost. Peter came to see differently in time."

"What happened, Ruth?" Lois asked eagerly. "I knew there had been some great disappointment in your life. Mother hinted that you came very near to being a close relative to us."

"Peter left me and went out to New Zealand. I never gave up praying for him. I wear his picture here, next to my heart," I confided, drawing out a little locket with Peter's picture.

"Did you never see him again?" Lois questioned.

"No, he did come to know Christ later through an accident abroad. He did not let us know that he lay long months in hospital where he had time to think. A letter came telling me the good news of his conversion. We planned our wedding to a detail, but Peter died before we ever met again. All of his letters have been preserved, and you write so like him,

Lois. But enough of my own story. Have you told Glyn that you could not consider his proposal because of the unequal yoking?"

"Yes, I tried to, but he would not listen. He pleaded his cause eloquently and refused to take back the diamond until more thought had been given to the subject. I held out no hope to him, but you can see how he feels my decision could blight his entire life. His success or failure, his ultimate salvation or rejection—is the responsibility of that to rest upon my shoulders?"

"No, God never intended you should carry so heavy a load. Yours is only to listen to His command and to obey. The responsibility is with God. He has never, never let anyone down who trusted in Him. Isaiah says, 'Thou shalt hear a voice behind thee saying, This is the way; walk ye in it.' James says, 'If any of you lack wisdom, let him ask of God, that giveth to all men liberally, and upbraideth not; and it shall be given him.' I have claimed those promises in more than one situation. God cannot fail a trustful, childlike soul when they ask guidance of Him in so important a life-decision."

"You will pray for me as I seek to sincerely know the will of the Lord?" Louis asked earnestly. "How easy it would be to let one's human love direct one's decision in such an important matter. I wish to study the Scripture on this subject—not just an isolated text or two." Lois looked at her watch and knew she ought to be leaving for "Sunny Mount."

We walked slowly down the steps and on to the lawn. As I watched Lois wave and walk out of sight, I noticed an air of sweet womanliness that made her more winsome than ever. Why did it have to happen to Lois and break her heart? Upon deeper reflection, I knew that suffering could only make the submissive soul to shine more lustrously in the diadem of the Crucified Lord. It was part of His polishing process with His redeemed diamonds. There was no chance about this happening—it was part of His purpose. I sat down in the lounge and let the darkness cover me as memories sweet and sad filed past me. I was aroused from my reverie by Glyn's return. He declined any supper, and retired to his room after thanking me for all my past kindness to him.

CHAPTER NINE

THE GREATEST GEM DEAL

"Sunny Mount" was all astir with wedding preparations when I left for London. How uneventful had been our lives until Glyn had come that July afternoon, almost a year ago!

Mrs. Stanford and I both had set aside time for special prayer for Lois and Glyn. A few minutes before leaving for London, Lois had managed a hurried conversation with me. "I'm glad you're going, Ruth, though I'll miss you terribly. Glyn needs you. I'm afraid of his doing some foolish, rash act he will regret a life time, for I cannot feel I can give him the answer he wishes. I have asked God for wisdom to know how to pray only for His glory and that Glyn's life may be yielded to the King."

A little note from Mrs. Stanford came in the mail, telling me Lois had reached a conclusion, but not without it taking its toll in sleepless nights and loss of appetite. "Since writing Glyn," Mrs. Stanford wrote, "Lois has had a calm, serene and quietly cheerful manner. She has thrown herself into helping Carey sew and pack. We're praying earnestly for Glyn that Lois's holding to Bible principle on this question will not adversely affect him."

I learned how Lois had written, from Glyn himself. Dr. Burns was the bearer of the valuable little parcel—the diamond and the letter. Glyn had not been at home when he called. I had placed the parcel on his desk in the library with his other mail, but I awaited his arrival with a degree of dread. I didn't see anything of him that night, and he went off to work the next morning without breakfast.

The following evening in the lounge, Glyn handed me the letter. "Want to read it? She's written a little sermon where I expected a warm return of love." He stood looking out of the window, his back to me, as I read:

Dear Glyn:

I have entrusted the lovely diamond into Dr. Burn's care, knowing that it would reach you safely. Thank you for showing it to me and sharing its history with me. I am so sorry to have to hurt you by returning it, but I cannot retain it on the conditions you stipulated.

My answers to you that day in Glasham were so incoherent, that I am glad you gave me the opportunity of setting down in black and white the product of careful and tearful thought. You took me so by surprise that day; I was dreadfully confused and unintelligible. Why must I cause you pain, Glyn? I have asked that "why" over and over again. You have done nothing to deserve the torture which I have to inflict; you have showered us with so many kindnesses that I am deeply indebted to you. I should be the last to cause you heartache. Only because I would need to grieve sorely Someone else I love more dearly, do I take up my pen.

You have asked me—in diamond language—to accept a setting of your own choosing. You are asking me to become yours. That I cannot do for I belong to Someone else already. I was bought with a price, the precious blood of Jesus. I am really not my own to give away. You must seek the permission of my Lord and Master. If I were to accept your offer for some beautiful, luxurious setting for my life, I would doubtless not hear Christ say: "And they shall be mine in that day when I make up my jewels."

However, by far the most effective argument you used, I can now answer. It caused me the most pain for it sounded so plausible and appeared to be just what I would like to have done for you: namely, to ever be with you, helping you to be a better man and encouraging you to always choose wisely. But you have delegated to me a task which no human being was meant to fulfill. The only Perfect Gem is the Lord Jesus Christ. He seeks to come into every heart and is pictured as knocking at the door of every person. He is hurt because you do not admit Him, and because you are looking to some poor human to be to you wisdom, strength, and decision. He couldn't possibly bless our lives together when you have so ignored Him.

In the first place, being only human, I am capable of error. You could be terribly disappointed in me in time, but never would you be with Christ, the Sinless and Spotless One. I could be suddenly snatched from your side by death or illness. He never leaves us nor forsakes us. You are asking me to occupy His rightful place. Can't you see how disloyal I should be if I accepted your offer, and how untrue I would be in the end to your best interests if I did not show you how serious it is not to take the Lord Jesus Christ into your life?

I have studied my Guide Book and the command is plain: "Be not unequally yoked together with unbelievers." A vital question the Good

Book asks is this: "Can two walk together except they be agreed?" Your love for me would brighten so much, but unless you loved Christ and owned Him as Lord, you would constantly be irritated at my placing Him first in my affections. I should want daily to take time for communion with Him; you would not understand. I should like daily to study the Bible, patterning my life by its precepts; you would not own His commandments as binding for your life and again there would only be pain and confusion. I should seek to bring erring ones to Christ; you would be wanting me to go somewhere with you instead. We would be unequally yoked, pulling in different directions, totally misunderstanding one another. Such frustration would eventually occasion you much greater pain than this present decision.

I hope you do not think I am writing this unfeelingly. No one I have ever met has called forth the spontaneous affection that you do. If you only loved my Master, I am sure we could render much more effective service together, and so happily! We have so much else in common—our love for Africa, our love of nature and books, our similar tastes on so many lines. And then, you could supply what I have missed all my life—a father's or brother's manly love and protection. The day you drove me to the hospital, I realized your quiet strength in times of need. But you, too, have so missed a good woman's tender affection. Oh, Glyn, I can only pray for you!

The way ahead looks difficult for you, for I know that you would never become a Christian for personal or selfish reasons. And to be truly born again, there must be the acknowledgment of sin against God. You must want God for Himself and for no other reason. Apart from any thought of me, I pray you may become His child and know true happiness. If ever I can help you toward this goal, short of compromising my convictions, I should be so happy!

Yours most sincerely,

He folded the letter tenderly and placed it back in his wallet. As he did so, I noticed that he had managed to procure a photo of Lois which he kept under the transparent covering.

"Pretty tough on me," he said as he pushed the corner of the rug up with his foot, and then straightened it again. "She's driven me further away from religion. I warned her that it would be so. It's God Who won't let her do it. She loves me, and but for her fanatical notions about religion, she would be mine. If I got 'born again' as she calls it, I would be doing it to get Lois, which I would never do; and, if I don't get 'born again' I never can have her. It's hopeless. There's no chance for bargaining—only full surrender," Glyn added bitterly.

I had thought of Glyn as being heart-broken, but I had not calculated on this bitterness. Now I saw walled-up barriers of ill-feeling, not toward Lois but toward God.

"You've no idea how staying around these parts seems impossible now," he confessed. "I've thought, perhaps, it's time to pick up and carry on the business somewhere else."

"You will remain at least for Dick and Carey's wedding, Glyn?" I begged. "They would miss you—and Lois? She would feel it, too. It's only five or six weeks off."

He made no promises, but he made no apparent preparation for leaving either. The days that followed were difficult and trying ones. He needed the only One Who could heal broken hearts and he was turning his back upon Him. Prayer, united prayer, was requested for him, and the Marchants joined us, and how we did pray!

*** *** * * * * * *

The wedding is now a thing of the past. It would have been a huge event in Bradleholme, but it was just a minute ripple upon London's ocean of humanity. Larch Memorial Hall had been chosen because it was of such easy access to most of those who had been invited. Dick and Carey had wished to fulfill the Scriptural injunction, "When thou makest a feast, call the poor, the maimed, the lame, the blind; and thou shalt be blessed." So a willing band of young people had spread out through that crowded area with personal invitations to the wedding.

Responding to the invitations were Teddy Boys, factory girls, elderly women, middle-aged women, and those men who could get off work. Histories of sorrow and sin were written on many a countenance. We, the friends, were scattered throughout the audience. Hawes was represented; Bradleholme friends were there as well as Carey's circle of friends and Dick's acquaintances; friends of the Marchants of many years standing, as well as new-found connections—Amyenne Manvers and Glyn—all were there to celebrate this happy occasion.

Dr. Burns gave Carey away, and her very simplicity was her greatest attraction. Dick looked radiantly happy and so handsome. The hall was filled with the fragrance of banked up flowers. Glyn had not stinted money, and Pauline had not spared time in decorating.

Now and again the audience moved a little restlessly as Dick's father gave the message, but on the whole the attention was surprising. This man of God believed that every event should be used purposefully in getting the "good news" to every creature. Since the message altered the course of several of the chief characters in my story I trust you will forgive me for giving a brief synopsis of it here.

How fatherly Mr. Marchant seemed as he beamed upon the audience and gave his opening remarks:

"I've been wondering, what were your thoughts as this simple but affecting ceremony has been enacted. I think I could turn prophet and tell you almost to a person. You young men directed your thoughts to some little woman you love, and whom you hope one day to lead to the altar. Some of you young girls have been thinking, 'When will he pop the question and ask me to marry him?' Some others have an ideal perhaps not yet realized, and you wondered whom you will finally meet and marry.

"There are, doubtless, others of you who have loved ardently and deeply only to have your love spurned. You have had bitter thoughts, anxious thoughts. You older ones have had tears in your eyes as memory recalled the time when you stood before the minister or registrar and said a joyful 'I will' and then started life with happy plans and golden dreams. For some of you, death has come and rudely, without your permission, snatched away that loved one. Others have had something worse than death come in—sin has stealthily entered your partnership and robbed you of its joys. Drink has claimed the better portion of your partner's money and attention, or unfaithfulness—the entrance of a third person—has come and given you the jealous, bitter, revengeful feelings. Yes, SIN has dealt the worst blows of all. But there are still others here who have sat with happy recollections, for you are walking hand in hand, perhaps with the silver in your hair, down the hill of life. The shadows are beginning to fall, but a stronger bond unites you now than when you stood at the threshold of married life and commenced your journey together.

"There is One Who has been present here this afternoon Who has had thoughts toward you and me beyond our comprehension. He seeks a life partnership with each one of us, a partnership which, if entered into, cannot help but end successfully. He has already thoughtfully prepared a home—a mansion—and His love is beyond compare. Hear His voice and behold His attitude of pleading: ' Behold I stand at the door and knock; if any man hear My voice and open the door, I will come in to him and will sup with him and he WITH ME.'

"But first, I want to tell you my business today. I am a matchmaker for God. Long years ago, a certain servant was sent by a very wealthy man on an errand of great importance. He sought a wife for this man's young son, and it was a vital matter that he should find the right woman. This servant was a man of God, and he prayed that the great God would guide him to such a woman. At the end of his day's journey, while at the well of that eastern city, he met a beautiful girl, and upon talking to her and observing her, he found her to be courteous, hard-working, kind, and dutiful. Her parents put a question to her that I would like to put to each one of you. It is found in the Bible in Genesis 24:58: 'Wilt thou go with this man?'

"Today, as God's servant, on behalf of my Master's Son, I ask that same question. In all fairness, I must tell you what my Master's Son is like. Remember, this is a proposal, and each one of you will have to answer 'yes' or 'no' before this service is over. This could be your wedding day as well! Don't you ever say nobody ever proposed to you! Well, I am sent by a King and it is His Son Who has asked me to put this question to you: 'Wilt thou go with this man?' Of course, before giving your answer, some of you who do not know much about Him, will want to know what He is like. Let me tell you.

"Firstly, He is loving. Carey would never have married our Dick, had she not been assured that he loved her. 'We love Him because He first loved us,' said one who went into a similar partnership with this Man, Christ Jesus. No one ever loved you like He does. Will you not give your answer in the affirmative to such a Lover of your soul? One such partnership was made, and the man said later, 'And to know the love of Christ that passeth knowledge.' It passes knowledge, the love of This One for you.

"Secondly, this Man Who is asking for your heart and hand is a wonderful Provider and His strength is amazing. He promises to supply all your needs. Carey said 'Yes' to Dick because she knew he would partner her in the dark hours and work for her. Now if everyone here knew how lovely Jesus is, none would hesitate to say, 'I will go with this Man forever.' You need someone strong, friends, when you are weak and helpless. You need a protector in time of storm and stress. You need a friend like Jesus when others forsake and misunderstand.

"Oh! the broken-hearted people there are today because they have never had such a life partner. They are alone, tempest-tossed, disillusioned, helpless, and worn with battling against life's odds. They expected too much from human beings, but they have never partnered with Christ.

"Let me tell you a few more wonderful things about Him. He is the Prince of Peace; partner Him and you will have the Peace-Maker always with you. He is a Specialist, too; no one can bind up broken hearts and heal sick bodies like this Man of Calvary. Think of having Him always at hand! Then, He helps those He partners to break any vicious habits. He is called a Counselor as well. Are you in perplexity? He will guide you through life's mazes with amazing skill. He knows the intricate pathway through life for He is a Guide; He is a Light, and if we partner Him we shall never walk in darkness; He is a fountain of Life, and so if we thirst, He has the living water. He has rest for the weary, strength for the faint; and love, matchless, amazing love for the unloved. Who would not partner such a Man? Will you go with this Man, Christ Jesus? He is listening just now for your answer.

"My third and last point: He has sacrificed much for you. Let us suppose that Dick had rescued Carey from a burning building or a watery grave. She would have doubly loved him for his risking his life for her. Now, this Prince of Peace did more for you than that. God was angry with every one of us, so angry that all of us would have had to go to Hell. But this God-Man stepped down and said, 'I will take the punishment for all so that all may go free.' 'For God so loved the world, that He gave His only begotten Son, that whosoever believeth on Him should not perish but have everlasting life.' Such love—such sacrifice! Death cannot sever this partnership. It is not only 'till death do us part,' but throughout the endless ages of eternity. Moreover, He has a beautiful home prepared for us and will come again and receive us unto Himself that where He is there we may be also. Who will go with this Man?

"Let us in closing just remember again the words of the verse I quoted at the very beginning. 'Behold I stand at the door and knock.' He is making His proposal. How badly you have treated Him! You have rejected Him. You have slighted Him. You have told Him, 'some other time.' Your sin is very great—there is no sin as black as the sin of saying 'no' to this Knocker, for He holds the key to Eternal Life. He is the Way across the black gulf of death to Eternal Life. Repent and believe the good news. If you have viewed the spotless purity of this Man Who seeks you, doubtless you have felt your utter unworthiness. You have glanced down at the sin-soiled garments your soul is wearing and shrank from the unsuitable attire. You have seen every spot of dirt; the rents that sin has made. You cannot possibly meet Him in these garments, filthy with sin's defilement. This, too, the King has made a provision for by offering a wedding garment—the white robe of forgiveness. Your objection there cannot stand.

"'Wilt thou go with this Man?' What is your answer to be? 'Yes?' The marriage of a soul could occur at this precious time of the marriage of my son and his young bride. Will you open quietly the door of your heart? Will you say, 'Yes,' to this amazing Lover? 'Wilt thou go with this Man?'

"Will not someone here this day perfect this happy event by making a life decision?"

At this, to our surprise, Amyenne Manvers rose decisively and walked forward. Instinctively everyone bowed his head as Mr. Marchant sent up a touching prayer that moved the audience, accepting this open declaration as a perpetual sign and seal of her union with the Lord Jesus Christ.

The strains of the organ played as the audience filed out and congratulated the bride and groom. The reception was to be held in an adjoining building.

Nata and Sheila joined Lois and myself. It was evident that her life had blessed these two. But Nata had some news to impart: "You may think, Lois, that the C.I.D. squad have been rather slow in their findings, but we have all been at work. Have you heard the latest? Judith Armstrong skipped the country with Leonard McAllistair. She evidently had run up some huge bills at several large London draper shops, and things were closing in on her. They have since married, we understand. Poor Judith—what an ending to a most promising career—everything seemed in her favor."

"How sorry I feel for her," Lois exclaimed sympathetically. "Leonard McAllistair? Remember, Ruth," Lois said, turning to me, "the one who insulted me at the Manvers' Christmas party?"

"Her people are terribly upset about it all," Nata explained, "and so is Miss Drake. Mary Gryson, her little shadow, is lost without her. Mrs. MacRoberts has questioned Mary quite a bit. She owned up to taking the pink notepaper, at Judith's suggestion. She also took a page of your letter, but she had given this also to Judith. Sheila, Evelyn, and I went to Miss Drake and related our findings."

Sheila interposed, "Did you know that Audrey Castleton got the job at the new center? It is a shock to everyone for she is so young, and then she has not had experience in any of the other centers first. Miss Drake acts if the bottom has fallen out. We do feel sorry for her."

"We all wish we had someone like you back again. We three try to keep up the prayer and Bible study, but we miss you terribly," Nata admitted.

We had by this time entered the building where the reception was to be held, and so our group was broken up as we were shown to our seats. Everything went off beautifully. I looked around for Glyn, but he had already gone to the car and was waiting in a most thoughtful mood. As we drove home, I told him what the C.I.D. squad had discovered. He had not heard as yet about Judith and Leonard, but said he was not surprised. He did not comment upon the wedding, and to me it soon blended into one of those pleasant memories that belong to the past.

*** *** * * * * * *

Lois and her mother returned to "Sunny Mount" where Mrs. Stanford continued to improve. I never lacked work and Glyn went about his business in a deeply serious frame of mind. We noticed he did not eat much, and he was difficult to engage in conversation. In the evenings he shut himself up in his library; and the household staff, as well as myself, grew alarmed about this once so naturally cheerful young man.

This could not go on, so one evening I ventured to knock on his library door. It was a tiny bit ajar, and as no one answered, I stepped inside. Glyn was sitting with his head in his hands.

"Are you all right?" I asked. "You have eaten nothing today. Are you sick?"

He still did not look or answer, and stepping closer I could see that his shoulders began heaving and his strong frame shook as the tears ran down to the floor. I sat down quietly nearby and waited. I have never before known him to shed a tear. He was not sentimental. I had seen him quiet, morose, uneasy, bitter, self-assured and light-hearted, but never weeping. I doubt if he had cried since Kathryn's death.

"Isn't there something I can do for you, Glyn?" I questioned.

"No one can help me where I am now," he informed me despairingly. "I've tried everything. I've even tried Church. I only seem further off from the goal."

"Let me read you something from God, Himself, in His Word," I ventured. "In that Book, He has told us the solution to every problem of life." I left to get my Bible, and returning I turned to the 15th chapter of Luke. How helpless one feels standing in the presence of a convicted soul! How careful one must be lest one interfere with the work of the mighty Holy Spirit and so mar the perfect work He always brings to a finish! I read slowly the stories of the lost sheep, the lost coin, and then the prodigal. I could not tell whether he was listening or not, but when I reached that verse: "I will arise and go to my father, and will say unto him, Father, I have sinned against heaven, and before Thee, and am no more worthy to be called Thy son," I stopped and said to Glyn, "Do you acknowledge yourself to be a sinner, Glyn? God says, 'If we confess our sin, He is faithful and just to forgive us our sin and to cleanse us from all unrighteousness.'"

"That's just the trouble," he responded. "I have sinned."

"Then we can read on," I said. "This story tells the way home to God." And I read: "But when he was yet a great way off, his father saw him, and had compassion, and ran, and fell on his neck, and kissed him."

"'A great way off. . .' Read that part again, Ruth."

I read the passage over, and when I again reached that place, "But when he was yet a great way off. . ." Glyn interrupted me.

"Stop! That's where I am," he said, "'a great way off.' I couldn't have expressed the way I feel just now better than by those four words. Let me read them for myself, Ruth," he requested.

Finding the place, he read silently and thoughtfully. "This my son was dead, and is alive again; he was lost, and is found." Then followed a tense pause of some minutes.

"Dead—alive; lost—found. That's me, Ruth. I've come home, and God and I have made it up. We'll stay together for life and work together. You know," he exclaimed, "that story is real, for I know what it feels like to get up in a temper and leave home. But, it's worse when a man has picked a quarrel with the Almighty. My, I'm glad! I didn't know such joy could come to one in this life-time," he said, rising from his seat and walking up and down the room. There was a glow on his face that betokened the inward change. There was a glint in his eye that revealed understanding. He freely talked of the weeks of suffering, of anxiety, of bitterness finally ending in despair—and then this! Seed sown in his heart as a child had lain dormant until touched by loving hands, and watered by faithful ministers.

"That story ends with a feast," I suggested. "You've not eaten properly for weeks. I am going to prepare you a proper meal."

It did not take me long to inform the Marchants and Stanfords of the remarkable change which had transpired in this life. Glyn, a determined man in all other things, was no less so now in the matters of the soul. He shamed many Christians of years of standing. I saw a new Bible on his desk and he assiduously read it. Evening family prayer was instituted by him, for he had known father and me, and the Stanfords, to have regularly observed this ceremony. But Glyn longed for spiritual companionship, and he was to find new light and help again through the ministry of Mr. Marchant.

Glyn had tried several places of worship, but he felt most at home and received most benefit spiritually at Larch Memorial Hall. The services were beautiful for reverence, and grand for their simplicity; it exactly suited the type of hearers gathered there.

Not long after that was one Sunday service which marked another era in Glyn's spiritual experience. "Again, the kingdom of heaven is like unto a merchant man, seeking goodly pearls; who, when he had found one pearl of great price, went and sold all that he had, and . . . bought it." How very appropriate this subject was for this young jewel merchant, sitting beside me. "All other pearls," Mr. Marchant had said, "goodly though they might be, are to be laid at His feet that we might possess the Pearl of Greatest Price." The entrance fee was nothing; the cost of discipleship was everything. Christ would reign in our hearts on no other terms than those of full surrender. Sinful self was the fearful rival of this kingly Monarch, and one or the other must rule on the throne of our hearts. All other gems must be exchanged for the Pearl of Greatest Price!

So it was that the following week Glyn weighed most seriously the greatest gem deal he had ever transacted. Diamonds, worth thousands of pounds, had passed through his hands, but this deal had to do with "the Pearl of Great Price." He told me afterwards that he went fully over all his goodly pearls, considering it as a business transaction, and "for joy" decided in favor of the One Pearl. It seemed the only sensible thing to do. Heavenly investments would never pass away. I wished so often that Lois could have witnessed the change in him. However, he never contacted Lois, for he seemed to feel that he must prove up.

One evening, not long after this, Glyn said he had quite a few plans to lay before me. We went into the library. I looked into his face as the late August sun shone into the windows. It was a chastened, humble, but no less determined man that I saw.

"Ruth," he explained "I'm going back to Africa. I startle you, I can see by your undisguised surprise. I have not been able to settle since the night I came to the Father, and the conviction has grown upon me with each passing day that the job I'm doing here is no longer His will for me."

I slowly nodded, and he continued: "The resolution in the story of the prodigal has not been fully carried out in my life. I have arisen and been accepted by my Heavenly Father . . . but my earthly father?" Here he stopped and looked at me. "I have sinned against him, too. I, also, asked one day for my portion. I, too, went into a far country. In the light of the highest values, I wasted my talents and time, too, in riotous living—being entertained and entertaining. Thank God I had not spent all yet, but I need to ask for his forgiveness, too."

"You could write and ask that, Glyn," I argued.

"Yes," he replied. "I conquered that temptation. It's the easier way out. No, I must arise and go to my father and say . . . 'make me as one of thy hired servants.' I have amends to make. I blamed father and mother for so much, but I never showed love to them as a son should. My father longed for my companionship in business. I left him, because I thought he had failed me as a child and then wanted to run my life as a young man. I have been utterly selfish—abominably so! I must shine out the life of my Partner, and in my own home I must testify to His saving grace.

"The opportunities in the nearby vicinity are unlimited. I came here to be free to do my own will; now I am a willing love-slave for life. I came in search of a human diamond and I have found the Pearl of Greatest Price. My quest is accomplished and now my life term of service must begin to prove my gratitude and loyalty."

"You talk as if you intended to leave Britain for good?" I questioned.

"For how long I do not know. There is much that is dear to me here, and I dare not consider it until I have finished my task, and hear my Master's clear direction otherwise. Will you keep 'Wren Glen' for me, Ruth? At least, keep it open until my way is clearer? You have cheerfully acted as my agent in other matters; think it over."

"When do you go?" I asked.

"The sooner the better," he answered firmly. Once my mind is made up, I see no reason for delay. I have booked a plane seat in two weeks' time. I delayed telling you until all plans were well formulated.

There is pain in leaving you, for you stand for so many precious associations I have had here. You were a better expert in gems than I was, Ruth."

"And . . ." I choked, "you will not see the folks at Bradlehome again?"

"No, I think not. I have much to do to wind up all my business in the small amount of time I have left myself. Besides I would only embarrass the Stanfords. It seems so beastly of me to have put such rigid tests to others. I didn't see myself as I do now. I must prove my loyalty and stand the tests of the Master Cutter upon my own life. I am a poor, rough, uncut, unpolished diamond, in no way equal to those I have so critically and at first even cynically watched. There is so much to be endured and sacrificed before I could dare lay claim to Lois Stanford. I, too, am now at the disposal of Another. I am not my own any longer. I stand by for orders."

"I am sure Lois would have loved to have seen and talked to you as a Christian," I suggested.

"I have set my face towards Jerusalem—Africa—and how am I straitened until it be accomplished. Don't tempt me back to an easier pathway or I should have to say, 'Get thee behind me, Satan.'" And he laughed. "No, Ruth, I know you would never tempt me to an easier course. I don't dare allow myself to be so tried.

"But," he continued, "don't ever feel sorry for me. Remember the wedding sermon. I have a Life Partner. I have the perfect Gem always near me, and my standards shall be set by His example and His Word to me."

Our evening supper had been served, and we left the conversation just there. I was stunned, but time doesn't stand still for us while we're getting adjusted. Glyn's farewell took place with little fuss; it was hard to realize that he was leaving for Africa. I could make him no final promise regarding staying at "Wren Glen" until I had made arrangements about "Mountain View."

A letter from Mrs. Stanford requesting my help in deciding some questions took me to "Sunny Mount" sooner than I had planned, and how good it was to see my lovely friends again. Lois had written, but avoided any mention of Glyn, so I hadn't been able to ascertain what she felt regarding his recent behavior. I tried to explain to them the surprising change of outlook which resulted in his deciding to return to Africa. Mrs. Stanford told me that Lois could not hide her anxiety to once again meet Glyn. She watched the mail wistfully. She would start when the milk or grocer's van pulled up. Why had he not tried to contact her when all the barriers had been removed?

I explained Glyn's feeling of unworthiness. He had recognized the stubborn will that had always dominated his life, and he was in a process. He had written briefly and I shared his letter with the Stanfords.

"Arrived home in good form. Walked in as though it were a daily occurrence. (I hate fuss, welcome parties, and publicity). Mother was surprised and overjoyed. Father, as usual, was quiet. However, mother's pride has been offended as she sees that although perhaps more dutiful and submissive, I can't bend to her capricious desires as much as formerly. She cannot tolerate my religious enthusiasm and as I have laid my plans before her for trying to help the African in all my spare time from father's business, she has been extremely upset. She informs me that her circle think I have religious mania. They believe I am wasting my life and hint that perhaps some sorrow or scrape I experienced in Britain has affected my mind. So I know a sort of pity and isolation from this circle. Gradually I am beginning to make new friends and acquaintances. Father is softening towards me more and more, and I believe he will be won yet."

Another short letter followed in which he took up an item of business regarding "Wren Glen," and I share a part with you.

"I am seeking to break down a stubborn will which has dominated me all my life. Submission to the initial processes that a diamond must undergo is not so easy. Is it crushing and screening? I wonder. It feels like it at times, but it so different with the Perfect Gem always within view. The partnership is grand, but I am a dull mate I fear. The task of becoming disciplined is not easy.

"Perhaps you will not know what it cost me to leave London when so much I loved was centered nearby. I did not consult my own desires lest I take an easier course. Pray for mother—she's already prying me for any secrets. She is doubtless planning my future. Gratefully, Glyn."

The letters were eagerly devoured by Lois. They satisfied her mind regarding Glyn.

CHAPTER TEN

DIAMONDS COME TO LIGHT

We sat around the little table after the evening meal, slowly sipping our tea and discussing our future plans.

"Well, what next, Mrs. Stanford?" I questioned. "We've had a year of momentous changes and it's rather hard to accustom ourselves to the daily, dull routine."

"We can't live on like this, mother," Lois said. "It was all right when you were ill, but now I am merely loafing."

Just then the butcher's van drew up, and her mother stepped out to do some purchases.

"Mother doesn't realize just quite how it is for me. I just can't continue like this. The A.B.S. have been good, but I can't take advantage of them now mother is around doing many of the jobs herself. I need some good work to do.

"Pauline wrote saying they were wishing for another worker; one that could accompany her in her visitation. They would be glad to pay a small salary. This is up my street, and I could perhaps arrange time for continuing my language studies."

"Is this your first choice, Lois?" I asked.

"No, I couldn't say it would be my first—at least it wouldn't have been a week ago, but it is today. Now I'm perfectly happy and contented in this choice. I feel I could lose myself in such an effort."

"Why lose yourself?"

"'He that loseth his life shall find it,' Christ said. You know, Ruth, I was looking forward to the greatest happiness I had ever known when Glyn became a Christian. I thought, you see, that we would live happily ever after. I'm afraid I rather built up on it because he was so determined before. When he didn't even bother saying one word to me before going, I was a little hurt. A readjustment was necessary. I felt I had been let down. All my contacts with him were before his conversion—not a chance to see him afterwards.

"After a little studying of the Guide Book it became evident that I had thought God ought to guarantee me happiness because I was a Christian. Without realizing it, I suppose I figured that it was rather like an insurance against disaster or trouble. The disciples were filled with joy when following the pathway of duty and often when persecuted or jailed. Their joy was real and enduring because it was dependent on abiding in Him Who never changes, and not upon circumstances.

"I thought of the countless broken homes and unhappy marriages and then, again, of the many widows and unmarried women who are denied the privilege of partnership. It shamed me for wanting a guarantee of happiness. While I am faithfully performing some unpleasant duty, I am capable of the highest joy possible because of a drawing upon Christ momentarily. Circumstances have nothing to do with that. That lesson was learned at my 'University.'"

I saw a gladness on her countenance that made me know it was just not religious cant. Lois was incapable of that. I did wish things would work out for her and Glyn. I knew they would someday.

Mrs. Stanford returned, and we laid our plans for the winter months ahead. "Sunny Mount" would be closed; Mrs. Stanford would live with me at "Wren Glen," and I was delighted with the prospects. Lois would stay with the Marchants. Dr. Burns, who had retired because of ill health, was glad to become my tenant and occupy "Mountain View."

*** *** * * * * * *

Two uneventful years elapsed since Glyn's departure for Africa. All lived a rich, full life, performing small duties faithfully, endeavoring to make the years of patient toil ones in which the Master should not find us wanting. I turned to my writing and research work for another book. Lois worked harder than ever, filling every extra hour with language study. Mr. Marchant's brother, a professor, had undertaken further tutoring and found her an apt pupil. Pauline and she were a happy pair as they went forth into the worst of districts to seek the lost.

Mrs. Stanford entered into her children's labors and was the intercessor behind the scenes. It was during this time that she discovered an effective ministry. Having always been actively engaged until her illness, she now felt the need of something that would marshal what physical and spiritual resources she possessed. Studying the local papers she closely followed the news. Was there an accident? Was a child killed? She wrote both to the bereaved parents and the driver of the vehicle. Was it a tragic loss of husband or wife? Was it a fire or flood? Was there a sudden tragic happening? She would pray and then write a brief note enclosing a suitable tract, card, quotation, or poem, always assuring them of interest and sympathy and seeking to lead them to Christ. In many cases she received replies showing gratitude. Now and again the person requested a visit and prayer, and Mr. Marchant, Pauline, or Lois would try to fill the need. In this way, the semi-invalid managed to fulfill a useful bit of ministering to the current needs about her.

Glyn had written infrequently and then briefly. His letters were always cordial, and hopeful, but he said little of what he was doing. We all returned to "Sunny Mount" for a few weeks holiday in August. It was so good to be back in Bradleholme again. The little church had suffered much in the absence of Dick and the Stanfords and also Dr. Burns, who had not been able to be as active. Audrey had indeed caused confusion by her loud denunciations and sarcastic statements, undermining the confidence of the godliest persons in the church. The praying ones were driven to the back seats, where they watched helplessly for a time, the introduction of many questionable amusements and methods into the very sanctuary of God. "If the foundations be removed, what can the righteous do?" David had said. I asked the question likewise as I viewed the damage caused by one person over a period of time.

Although in London, Audrey had kept an eager eye on affairs here. Her ears were always ready to listen to chit-chat and gossip. During the past year she had been chosen to represent the Youth Group at a Convention in South Africa, and she came back equipped with slides and information which had given her an opportunity for deputation work. Bradleholme was, of course, glad to welcome so important a figure, and we attended her lecture.

After the lecture she had skillfully piloted Lois to a quiet part of the church hall and said, "I have some word for you about Glyn Forster." She watched Lois start.

"You perhaps know that I had a chance to visit Johannesburg, so took the time to look him up. He and I always were more or less confidential. He seemed at times so utterly lonely and misunderstood. I think he knew I could grasp his situation because I was not quite so extreme in my religious views."

Mrs. Stanford had watched Audrey's tactics and now joined the two just in time to hear Audrey say, "There's a brilliant, beautiful young woman—hm-m-m I would say twenty-fivish," and she raised her eyebrows. "She went everywhere with him. To see the one was to see the other. I saw the blue prints for a hospital, a school, and for what, I understand, were to be several darling little homes. One home is partially completed and the foundations are being laid for the others. Brenda is helping him to draw up these plans. I thought you ought to know, for at one time I fancied you took to him a bit. He showed an interest in you for a while, too, but it was because, being bored stiff, he found a diversion in your quaint and amusing ways. When I mentioned your name in front of Brenda and asked if he never heard from you, he colored so. He was really quite abrupt. Doubtless I blundered, mentioning your name in Brenda's presence.

"You would like Brenda," Audrey went on. "She's got wealth, background, education, and extremely good looks, and good taste in putting those looks to the best advantage. She's no snob; she's very, very approachable. I suppose that's why Glyn took to her. She's religious, but she doesn't overdo it. While having luncheon at Glyn's house, I noticed she managed his mother artfully," and Audrey laughed, throwing back her head.

Lois had come home crestfallen, for Glyn had written so little. This story might be the possible explanation for his waning interest.

"I long to get back to my work," she said as the days drew to a close. "I am happy there, listening to the problems and troubles of others." Our work beckoned us back into the city away from our sheltered and lovely village. Day again succeeded day—everyone much the same. Lois seemed more in earnest than ever, throwing herself more heart and soul into her work. She seemed now to care less about taking greater risks, and if there was a corner where danger was rife, there she was bound to be.

One week-end Lois related to us a most interesting call she had made. She had climbed the cement steps, the iron railings of which had been torn down and twisted. Bits of refuse—orange peel, cabbage leaves and crusts of bread—were strewn on the landings. Knocking at one of the doors, she was met by a slatternly looking woman in a dressing gown, who wanted nothing to do with her, and slammed the door in her face. As she stood dazed, the door opened again, and the woman apologized, saying that there was someone sick in there that might be glad of a visit. She was shown into a dark vestibule off from which opened five doors. This apartment had at one time been the home of a doctor, but neighborhood deterioration had set in, and each room was now occupied by a different family. The landlady ill-humoredly pointed to one of the doors and said, "You'll find her in there."

Lois knocked and entered a small, overcrowded room, where a woman lay on the bed, and one small child played at the fireless hearth. One fleeting glance at the visitor, and the woman turned her face to the wall. It was with difficulty that Lois got her to talk.

"You're Lois Stanford, aren't you?" the woman finally asked. "Do you remember me?"

The caller looked at the pathetic figure—the hair disheveled, and the face pale and marked with lines of suffering and sin. "Your face is familiar; let me think," Lois told her.

But before she could place her, the woman went on: "I almost hate you for finding me. But I'm in trouble and offered a prayer. Perhaps God sent you. I'm Judith Armstrong—remember the Youth Hostel?"

Lois felt pity well up within her heart for the wretched woman before her. She stooped and kissed her and then took the child upon her knee. "I'm so glad, Judith, that I am the one sent to help you. To give a hand to an old friend is a great privilege. Have you had anything to eat?"

A few dirty dishes were stacked in the sink, and a breadboard with some crumbs told of a past meal. There was little in the cupboards, so Lois went out and quickly brought some groceries. She soon had a fire in the grate, and the kettle steaming. She washed the child, tidied up, and then promised another visit.

It was the next day that Judith was ready to talk. "Can you listen to what I have to tell you, Lois? You've been so kind to me, and heaped coals of fire upon my head. I don't deserve your interest, but it was just like you. The girls always said you had a face to whom a person would turn when in trouble, and though I denied it then, I have lived to find the truth of it now.

"I did you a dirty trick, and it's been on my conscience ever since," Judith confessed. "Now I have the opportunity to get it off my chest. I wrote that letter which caused all the trouble and forged your name," she admitted gulping. "I hated you so because your life condemned mine. I seemed like one possessed, and I could not account for some of the bitter words and unkind acts. But, but, there was a stronger influence working behind me." At this point she became violently agitated; sitting up, she pointed an accusing finger at an imaginary Audrey. "Audrey Castleton was the evil craftswoman, and I was her tool. Poised, strong-willed, and better balanced than I, she merely used me to get her ends and attain her goal. You might have influenced me towards higher things had it not been for an inveterate love of popularity on my part, and that woman's wrong influence which helped tip the scales that were already heavy on the side of evil." After delivering this vehement tirade she sat back exhausted.

"That is not all. My parents were wrong. They indulged my every whim as a child; gave me my own way. They never crossed me, for I had a violent temper. They lived for the day when I would marry up the scale, settle down to a life of social engagements and charitable objects. When I took a girlish fancy to a young man already partly alcoholic, it was no wonder I came to this. I've drunk too—drunk to forget; drunk because I didn't want to be the odd one out. The fear of being different was always my trouble. But look where it's brought me."

"Where is Leonard?" I asked, inwardly shuddering as I remember the scene at Manvers'.

She looked about apprehensively. "He's left me, roaming the streets, no doubt hoping for something more to spend on drink. When one's money, clothes, and looks are gone—his friends disappear, too. One has time to think a lot. I am sorry, Lois, for my dirty deal. I've suffered too much to cry. I'm hard. Now, I've told you the bold outlines of my life and got the weight off my chest. The filling in of smaller details would be too sordid and take too long."

"Do your father and mother know of your whereabouts?" Lois questioned.

"No, they would never want to be disgraced. Father's position, you know. Mother was always a lover of the constant whirl of engagements. She is well-known in all the social circles. I am supposed to be abroad, and Leonard is supposed to be holding some position as an Army officer."

Lois left the house with mingled feelings—sad at heart to find such heart-breaking effects of SIN, but glad to know that it was leading someone back to see life's true values. These slums held secrets, and the more she learned of life's sorrows, the more she felt impelled by love to visit and show, to these needy souls, something of the living Savior of men.

As Lois had meditated on the sad case of Judith Armstrong, she revolted against that cheap brand of evangelism that merely displayed Christianity as a decision and not a new, dynamic divine life in the soul that prepared and equipped it for a warfare. What robbery to offer a soul a theory instead of life, a creed instead of a Person, a decision instead of a born-again experience! How unfair to an individual to ask him to sign on a dotted line as a recruit in the Army of the Lord, and not acquaint him with the privilege and necessity of knee drill and of Bible regulations and rules to be obeyed, and of sharp encounters with a terrible foe who was day and night seeking his destruction! Who was to prepare him for the self-denial and sacrifice that the obligations of witnessing demanded? We deplore the shallowness of modern Christians but we go on blindly producing more and more of the same brand. It was little wonder there are so many deserters from King Jesus' army.

Our religion is becoming the laughing stock of false cults who have the wisdom and courage to impose their demands upon their followers—and daring demands too! We are just a caricature of the powerful Christians who turned the world upside down.

*** *** * * * * * *

Mr. Marchant deftly dealt with the Armstrongs, and the result was a reunited family. Judith gave birth to another child, and from that time on two small grandchildren gladdened two lonely hearts in the Armstrong home. But Judith, upon returning health, determined not only to repent of the past, but to undo something of the damage if possible. Her father, upon being appraised of the foul dealing, undertook to make a report to the Committee and thus clear Lois's name of the imputations that had hung over it for so long. An apology was tendered to Lois. She was offered a position with the Youth Groups as and when she desired to work upon such lines again. How long could Audrey continue her role of duplicity after this discovery? But she was clever in playing the game, never openly deceitful, but always artfully gaining her ends, by the use of any or all persons who were in close proximity to her.

Lois became more and more engrossed in her work. The two-and-one-half years of calling had begun to yield some results. The women's meeting and Sunday Schools were overflowing. And Lois and Pauline were ever seeking the lost sheep in the worst haunts of sin. Late at night, these two were to be found risking life and limb. Policemen often urged them to move on, warning that there was real danger. But in their calling, they had become acquainted with a young girl, Phyllis. She had come to London from an excellent home; her parents thought her studying in some college. The love for dress had always held her captive, and, not being able on a limited allowance to dress as she liked, she had been taught the way to earn big money quickly. So down into this district she had come. Little by little, Lois learned the tactics of these owners of the brothels.

Cigarettes containing drugs were offered to these women, and as the appetite grew, both the drug sellers and the brothel owners were assured of their quarry, for in order to obtain the money for the drugged cigarettes, the girls needed extra money. Behind the street women lay a powerful combine—the dope ring. More than once, Lois sensed she was being shadowed, and her movements noted. But nothing intimidated these daring "angels" as they came to be termed by the inhabitants.

One night, these two enterprising, daring "angels" were patrolling their beat on an errand of mercy when a call reached them. It was the voice of Phyllis as she was being dragged against her will, down a dark, unlighted alley. Lois darted across the street and then remembered no more until she awoke in a hospital ward. The next day the newspapers ran a sensational story about "The Angel." Lois had been badly shaken up. Fortunately, a fractured wrist and a bad bump on her head were the extent of her injuries.

But in a palatial dwelling in London's suburbs, a remarkable scene was being enacted. I learned the details later and will give them as they happened.

Old Mr. Spencer-Morton had returned home from work the previous day to find a letter from his son in Canada, saying he had already begun investigations regarding the whereabouts of his sister, Eleanor. He pleaded with his father to forget old grievances and join him in the search. But old Spencer-Morton had thrust the letter aside with a gesture of impatience. Still it weighed so upon his mind that the usual nap which he snatched in his comfortable chair was denied him. His thoughts went back across the years. He slept little that night. The next evening upon his return from the office, Mr. Pearce, his companion and secretary, came in as usual to read the daily newspapers to the old man. the latter was in for a greater shock. After perusing stocks and shares and dividends, the old business man was definitely elated. His business was a success and he was made. The political situation was next surveyed, and then Mr. Spencer-Morton reached impatiently for the paper, unaware of the shock that awaited him

"Here let me glance at it," he muttered impatiently. "Seems there's no news worth reading in it tonight." He turned the pages until his attention was suddenly riveted on the photo of a young woman. Handing it back to Pearce, he demanded, "Read that. Her face reminds me of someone. See what it says about her. Probably a marriage or a divorce. And he reclined back in comfort in his large easy chair.

Pearce read the head-line: "COURAGEOUS WOMAN WOULD-BE REFORMER ASSAULTED."

"Last night at eleven-fifteen, on the corner of Wolgarth Street and Saddler Avenue, a young woman, Lois Morton Stanford, received slight head and wrist injuries when attempting to rescue an acquaintance from attackers. It ended in a free-for-all fight as 'The Angel's' defenders rushed up and mobbed the attackers.

"It appears that the Misses Stanford and Marchant are often seen patrolling their beat on errands of mercy, and so have gained the goodwill of the inhabitants. Miss Marchant says that when the three tall men quickly closed in upon her companion, others ran to defend her. The three attackers appear to have been left in a sorrier plight than 'The Angel,' and what might have happened but for police intervention no one can predict. Several were taken to hospital for treatment.

"'The Angel' seems to have had quite an interesting background. Her mother, beautiful Eleanor Spencer-Morton, thirty years ago startled London society when she withdrew from its fashionable circle to become a worker in the City Mission. The same daring spirit that animated the mother when she renounced a fortune and the goodwill of society seems to have had rebirth in her daughter. We understand the father became a foreign missionary and a well-known translator. This episode has led to an official inquiry into existing conditions which brought on this incident."

A deep sigh escaped the old man's lips as he reached out a trembling hand. "Give me that paper," he demanded brusquely. A prolonged second study of the girlish face was followed by a long pause.

"Hm-m-m, unusual. Silly thing to do, though. Like her mother," he mused in a faintly audible voice. A few more items were read, but Mr. Spencer-Morton was away in his thoughts. He did not sleep for some nights. He had no wife—she had been dead two years now—with whom to talk it over. He grew restless and irritable.

Three days passed, when Spencer-Morton suddenly broke in upon his usual newspaper reading and said, "Pearce, make inquiries tomorrow regarding 'The Angel' of whom you read the other night in the newspaper. The hospital would be able to give you some clue."

*** *** * * * * * *

Lois had her head in her books when Pauline excitedly broke into the room, exclaiming excitedly, "An old man insists on seeing you, Lois. He drove up in a posh, chauffer driven Bentley. Whoever can he be?"

Louis had no time to reply for, just then, a portly, elderly gentleman was shown in. He moved rather jerkily and toyed with the large gold chain which hung across his dark waistcoat.

"Am I speaking to Lois Morton Stanford?" he asked tersely. Lois nodded. "May I speak to you alone?" he asked.

Pauline dismissed herself as she deemed he appeared harmless. The old man looked over the top of his gold rimmed spectacles, as he inspected the young woman before him. Her arm was in a splint, but she was seated beside a lamp which shed its bright rays upon her papers and books. Her own face was partially shaded by the soft glow of the maroon lampshade. As he studied her, the lines of his face gradually softened.

"I was quite interested in your adventure as reported in 'The Evening Chronicle,'" he began. "Would you be so kind as to give me your version? I have reasons, very justifiable, for wishing to know the truth. Papers so often give only a very garbled report of the real event."

He placed his cane in a corner near his chair which was opposite Lois. Lois looked at him, and would have marveled at a stranger's audacity had there not been something in the old gentleman's whole demeanor that interested her. Could it be that he wished to make a donation to the mission work?

Lois related the story, with a little more detail about Phyllis than the newspapers had reported. The old man interrupted from time to time with a few questions, but always beckoned her to continue, all the while intently studying her face. The sternness in his own features gradually seemed to be evicted as a kindly, benign look took over occupancy.

"And your mother?" he wanted to know. "The newspapers say she was also engaged in this kind of work. Is she alive at the present?"

Lois assured him of her mother's well-being and he reached into an inner pocket and brought out a card. Handing it to her, he said, "You might like to know my name."

Lois looked at the card under the lamp. "No, surely not—not Spencer-Morton! Spencer-Morton!" she repeated. Looking up into his face, she asked, "You are my grandfather, aren't you?"

"I am that," he said gruffly, trying to hide the emotion that he felt mounting in his breast

Lois rose and went over to his chair. "Grandfather, why didn't you tell me that? Here we have been sitting talking ever so casually. I have longed so for a grandfather and grandmother all these years." She was sitting now on a low stool at his feet.

"Will you let me ring mother? Oh, dear, how happy she will be!"

"No, not tonight. I've already had enough excitement for an old man like me. I've got to get used to the idea of women folks that are my own. Give me time. Give me time," he said as he waved her down again to a sitting position, for she was already making for the telephone.

"Just sit down and tell me more about yourself. That's about all I can manage for one night. I'm an old man, you know, and I've got to get used to the idea of grandchildren. You are so overflowing with good spirits that you quite tire me. But go on, what have you been doing with yourself? Have you any brothers and sisters?"

Lois spent the remainder of the evening answering his questions and covering the gap that the separation had made. How loving and kind this grandfather of hers might have been had not these grudges and bitter feelings been the unlovely bosom companions of his! Even then, it was taking quite a time to unlimber, and he felt awkward as love sought to untie the bands that had bound his heart all these years.

In the days which followed, Lois was the one that was to help make the awkwardness less between her dearly loved mother and her newly acquired grandfather. This she did artfully and delicately for she saw in him something that had been starved. Wealth had not been able to purchase the love he had so desired. Former religious scruples had long since faded and he had been left with only the skeleton of the old grudge, gaunt and horrid in its aspect. When it had been embodied with a supposedly real cause, it had seemed justified, but for many years now it had been only a ghost to torture his quiet hours. Only pride had kept him from being the aggressive party in a reconciliation.

The rejected daughter was lovingly told to return to her old home, and grievances and grudges were forgotten and forgiven. Several weeks later, Lois stood in the bedroom that had been her mother's when she had been just her age. No one had ever used Eleanor's room, and no one had entered it—so Spencer-Morton had thought. But the old family nanny had over-ridden orders and weekly dusted the room. Always before leaving it, she had prayed that its former occupant might someday be restored. The large oil painting of Eleanor that had taken so prominent a place in the hall below had been hung up here so that nothing might remind the father of his banished daughter.

Lois stood in front of the life-size painting. Suddenly she became overwhelmed by the realization of the tremendous cost of her mother's renunciation. Her emotions had been mounting from the time she had entered this palatial home of her mother's youth. The spacious grounds, the elegant furnishings, and now this picture which showed so clearly the world in which her mother had moved, contrasted so sharply with the memories of the utter simplicity and the pinch of poverty her mother had accepted without a murmur.

"Thank you, God, for a mother who was willing to follow in Your footsteps; who likewise became of no reputation; who also became poor for Your sake," she murmured. "Help me to more nobly accept my lot without complaining."

Lois had left the door open and old Spencer-Morton had found her thus. "God has been so good to me, Grand-father," Lois had said. "What a mother I have had, and now I am to know the love of a grandfather as well." And she put her arms around his neck. "Why were so many good things in life so long in materializing?"

"The best things of life are always delayed. It is our own obtuseness many times that causes this, but we appreciate them more when they do come."

"Is it always true, grandfather?" Lois asked.

"Always," he replied, but he did not know what his granddaughter was thinking. He was not aware that there remained, for Lois at least, one more, longed-for human relationship to be added in her life in order to complete her circle of happiness.

CHAPTER ELEVEN

THE DIAMOND CLAIMED

While recuperating at her grandfather's, Lois had ample opportunity of studying more of the old home. In the evenings, she would coax him to tell her stories of the past, and so she pieced together the history of the family. Mr. Pearce was being cheated out of his usual evening job, for Mr. Spencer-Morton enjoyed hearing Lois read the newspapers to him. Before the week was up, Mr. Spencer-Morton was actually joining mother and daughter in the evening family devotions. All good things, however, need to give place to duty, and so Lois planned to return to her former work.

"I really am feeling fit for work again," she informed the family group one evening. "I think I've gotten over the ill effects of my encounter enough to enable me to rejoin Pauline."

Grandfather Morton eyed her seriously. "Just exactly what are you going to do with your life? Do you intend spending it all in work in the slums? Are you to be a career woman or . . . .?"

Lois glanced at her mother and colored slightly as her grandfather left his sentence unfinished, expecting an answer to his supposition. "You see, Grandfather," she began slowly, "my life has been a bit hit-and-miss according to others' viewpoint. I have had no straight-forward education beyond secondary schooling."

Mrs. Stanford interrupted her. "Father, her ambitions for further education were given up cheerfully and heroically when I was ill. She nursed me over a period of years. Then, she took over work in a Youth Hostel to be near me when I was undergoing surgery. Since my recovery, she has been doing some intensive studying of languages under private tutors and at the same time working in the City Mission with Pauline Marchant."

"What about accepting that opportunity now for special educational advantages?" he suggested. "I'll see you over the hurdle of finance."

"Earlier in my life," Lois explained, "I had hoped to become a doctor, but after mother's illness, I thought perhaps I was better qualified to do special translation work. Getting attractive Christian literature translated for young Christians of other lands is an urgent need. Reading matter is so very scarce and Communists have been quick to supply this whereas Christians have been so slow. On the other hand, it takes a long time to get a doctor's certificate," Lois added reflectively. "I've given a lot of thought to these things."

"What's wrong with five or six years of study?" the old man protested. "You're still young and have no attachments to hold you back," he added, surveying Lois. "Unless you have something else in mind, I see no reason why you should not begin to plan in real earnest." He toyed nervously with his gold chain and then asked, "Or, is there any young man in the picture?"

"There used to be—not now!"

"I had hoped to have you near me for some time," Mr. Spencer-Morton went on. "You would lack nothing, and I could help make up for the years of hard struggling. A girl gets nowhere nowadays without a degree. You would stand a better chance of meeting the right young man if you mixed in the proper circles. You couldn't hope to find a suitable young partner down in your sphere of work."

"But, Grandfather, I believe that God plans our lives. I am sure you would highly approve of the one a Higher Hand wisely chose for me. If it is in His will, we shall meet in just the place He designs me to labor. But, there, we can pray over the future training or education. We're in no immediate rush."

"You and your mother think it all out," her grandfather concluded. "I don't know all the ins and outs of your private lives. Let me know your decision later so we can plan for the next semester if that's the route you want to go."

What the Stanfords did not know then was that the doctors were very concerned about the health of old Mr. Spencer-Morton. He was a difficult patient, certain that he knew more than the doctors about his case and refusing to retire from active business. A few days after the conversation regarding further education, he took a slight thrombosis attack, resulting in a partial paralysis of the left side. Nobody tended him more faithfully than mother and daughter, and the affection between them deepened and grew.

Dr. Peden drew Mrs. Stanford aside one morning and said, "Cannot you prevail upon this determined old gentleman to get away somewhere for a time? With his heart condition, he just cannot stand up to the program he daily sets for himself, and he refuses to listen to medical advice. If you will work with me we might manage to persuade him to take a trip abroad."

"And," he continued, "I think that young daughter of yours looks like she ought to be getting a break as well. Mr. Spencer-Morton has asked me to give her a thorough check-up. Could she come round to my surgery some afternoon this week?"

Lois did, and the check-up revealed a terribly run-down condition which had affected the blood stream. The doctor strongly urged a trip abroad for both grandfather and granddaughter. After some days of continual hinting about taking a holiday abroad, the old man finally acquiesced for the sake of Lois.

First-class cabins were secured, and a long cruise planned on a luxury liner. To Spencer-Morton's mind, Pearce was indispensable so he was to accompany the old gentleman as traveling companion and secretary. The doctor, knowing finance was no barrier, had suggested a nurse be engaged so that no responsibility should rest upon the young shoulders of Lois Stanford. She had been losing weight rapidly, and all color seemed drained from her face. Intense application to her studies, and the unceasing toil into the late night hours on the city streets of London had taken their toll. Mrs. Stanford was urged to accompany the party, but she realized that her young daughter had a tighter hold upon the old gentleman's heart-strings and so would be able to do more with him if alone. She longed for quiet, after traveling and changing so much of recent months.

A day or two after they had sailed away, I received this letter from Glyn following a silence of months. "My work is interesting, and one must learn not to weary in well-doing. Prejudices here lie deep. Racial differences are engrained, and when one seeks to break down barriers, one finds obstacles looming like mountains. I have avoided becoming embroiled in politics, but this is difficult because labor for their spiritual well-being touches on things dangerously contingent upon politics. In view of the great need all around and the great undone, I feel ashamed to put down here any of my small attainments. I am a privileged partner to One Who has never let me down.

"I do want to mention a more personal matter, Ruth. I have thoroughly despaired of ever becoming worthy of the diamond with which you entranced me when in Bradleholme. The nearer I try to approach Christ-likeness of character the more unworthy I feel and the more wretched and horrid seem the years I have spent squandering character, time and money. I seem farther away with all my trying, from the man of God I had hoped to be within these years. The equal yoking looks impossible.

"Your news of the re-uniting of the Stanfords with Mr. Spencer-Morton first heartened me greatly—and then, I am afraid, it dashed my hopes even more. When in London, I entrusted the building of "Wren Glen" to Morton Building Society, and so came to know something of the old gentleman. He didn't lack means, and now the Stanfords' fortune will be made. I can no longer act as the hand within the glove of the A.B.S., or hope to offer Lois the place I had sought to give her. You see, my fortunes have altered considerably. Father took me into his confidence a few months back and told me his conscience was giving him a spot of trouble. It's a long story, but an early partner, through love for drink, foolishly sold out his rights in the diamond company for ready cash. I learned that his widow and children were almost penniless. Although the deal was legally right, the transaction wasn't morally so. After much persuasion, father decided to make some remuneration, and as a result of such restitution, our family fortunes and assets have been severely affected. So now, doubtless, with Lois an heiress, we are on unequal footing again. Hopeless, don't you see?

"Mother is off on a pleasure tour. She cannot settle long without excitement of some kind.

Yours in possession of the Pearl."

Several weeks later, I received this letter from Lois:

Dear Ruth:

The lovely salt air and the perpetual sunshine are having most beneficial effects upon both grandfather and me. Vitality has come back, oh so slowly, to us both. We spend hours on deck in the sunshine, and have even felt like playing some deck games. Only one thing has clouded this lovely trip for me. Mr. Pearce, who is twelve years older than myself, proposed to me the other day. It always hurts to hurt others, but life does seem ridiculously funny. The one I loved never wrote; the one I don't love hounds my footsteps and waits upon me as if I were a queen. I told him there was someone else whom I had loved, and I could never, never consider another. I don't think he will bother me again.

But you just could never guess who is traveling on this boat. I kept noticing a beautifully dressed and highly cultured woman watching me. Sometimes it was in the lounge and at others, on deck. We never spoke, but I so often saw her somewhere near. In spite of her beauty, she looked so bored and sad, that it was pitiful to watch her. I think we were on the ship fully ten days before an occasion arose which gave us an opportunity of speaking. She is a Mrs. Forster from Africa.

She came up to me while I was on deck, reading my Bible. Approaching rather apologetically, she said she had wanted to speak to me about her son who had some fanatical notions about religion. She asked me all kinds of questions. I have tried to be as kind as possible to her. Grandfather has had some conversation with her, too. I am sure she is Glyn's mother, judging from his description of her, and her description of him. What a pleasure lover! She is in on all the social, glamorous side of boat life—dancing, the cinema, card playing and gambling. Will write again in a few days.

Another letter from Lois: You can't possibly know my joy, Ruth, and the wonderful surprise I had while our boat stopped at the Cape. After luncheon, I had gone out on the deck again for a little relaxation in my deck chair. It was a warm day, and I had been reading. I must have dozed for my book had fallen from my hands. I awoke rather suddenly and was startled by a stranger at my side who had drawn his deck chair close to mine. He kindly picked up my book and handed it to me. His dark sun glasses hid his eyes, but I knew the forehead, the hair and the lips that smiled. Can you imagine my surprise to see Glyn Forster sitting next to me? I shook myself to know whether or not it was a dream.

After my first hearty welcome, however, I felt a barrier as I thought of Brenda. I smiled, I am afraid, rather awkwardly and must have been reserved in my manner for he observed: "You are not wholly glad to see me? I thought your first spontaneous response was one of joy? Now you are more diffident and reserved."

"I am very glad to see you, Glyn, for old-time's sake. You must remember that some years have elapsed and changes have doubtless taken place in each of our lives since we last spoke together. Do tell me all about yourself and what you have been doing. I've heard of some of your plans," I replied guardedly, thinking that he could gently break the news of Brenda to me.

"I thought my plans were all secret. I had not meant them to be revealed until the wedding day," he answered, his eyes sparkling with delight.

"Oh, I see," I returned retiring even more into my shell. "I did not mean to pry into your private concerns, but when are you to be married?"

"That depends entirely upon the answer the right little woman will give."

"She would be foolish not to accept you, Glyn. She seems in every way suited to you from reports I hear. I would love to meet Brenda."

Glyn looked puzzled. "Brenda? She's my cousin. I've told her all about you, and she's keen on meeting *you.* Whoever has upset you with all this nonsense about Brenda?" he asked, leaning over and laying his hand possessively over mine. Then his eyes flashed as a thought stuck him. "It isn't Audrey again, is it? She has caused endless trouble for you, Lois," he said indignantly.

I nodded. "Yes, I'm afraid it is Audrey. After visiting Africa and seeing you, she told me of your attachment to a beautiful young woman by the name of Brenda. How could I know she was only a relative and that you were not . . ." Ruth, I never finished that sentence for I looked into Glyn's eyes and read there what he had tried to tell me before. There had been insuperable barriers; now there were none. He did not need voluminous words to assure me that his love had never altered.

"Audrey has caused each of us some apprehension," Glyn commented after a long pause. "I'll never forget how I felt when I thought you and Dick were to be married, and then the relief when I discovered it was wrong information. Now that you know the truth about me, can you accept this little gift and always, always keep it?"

He had reached into his pocket and taken out a jewel case. "Can you accept this for keeps?" he asked eagerly. I nodded in the affirmative; my heart was too overflowing with joy to trust myself to words. I had had so many misgivings about Brenda, and had striven so hard to be submissive and accept the fact as a part of my life-time cross. Now that I had found out the truth, I was too overwhelmed to make a decent reply, but Glyn seemed satisfied. My hands were shaking as I looked at the little jewel case in my possession.

"Open it, Lois," he said with a voice of new authority and ownership.

I released the small catch, and there instead of Kathryn's diamond was a small gold key.

"Let me explain," Glyn offered. "This key opens a door to a perfect setting consistent with our profession of following Jesus. I have sought my blue prints from the Master Architect in His Textbook. I believe I have attained the mind of Christ, as nearly as imperfect man is capable of doing. When you become mine at the altar, that day you shall know the full meaning of the key. As to Kathryn's diamond: I knew from reading Scripture about costly raiment and pearls, that you would feel awkward possessing such a diamond for the sake of show or sentiment. Kathryn would have fully acquiesced, I knew, and so her diamond is invested in all that that key will open up to you.

"Your look tells me you want to know more, Lois. I will explain the absence of the diamond and the substitution of the key afterwards if you can trust me. We have so much else to talk of now. Would you like to know how I happened to join your ship at the Cape? Here, read my mother's letter:

Dear Glyn:

I have exciting news for you. At last, after all my years of attempted matchmaking, I have found just the right woman for you. She will meet all your requirements, I am sure, although she doesn't come up to all of mine. She is sweet, if not beautiful; she is tastily dressed, if not fashionable; she is educated, if not sophisticated; she is from a good family and will be left a comfortable fortune, if not fabulously wealthy.

More than once, she has shown me courtesies and kindnesses during my bouts of physical trouble. So, if she does not fully come up to my ideas of all that I should expect of a perfect woman, I am willing to overlook that fact. At times I wish I could get hold of her and put just a few touches to her hair style and add a few flourishes of make-up. Something, however, tells me that although she is very modest and sweet, she knows her own mind and would speak it.

You just MUST meet her, Glyn. Through deft and delicate questioning, I have become quite sure that she has no other serious attachments. I think there was someone in her life a short while back but it appears to have not been too serious. I have watched her, here on the boat, most skillfully and courteously ward off admiring aspirants for her attention. And Mr. Morton, her grandfather, assures me she has no fiancé to his knowledge. Can't you arrange to casually join the ship at the Cape and make her acquaintance? You could sail along the coast to Durban. Leave your beloved duty long enough to meet this one who, I am sure, was meant for you, Glyn. I should enjoy your company and am good at making introductions, as you know from the past. Do obey me just this once. You will never regret it. Her name—I almost forgot that—Lois Stanford.

As I finished it, Glyn laughed and said, "You see, my mother is true to my description. She is still matchmaking, and for once I shall gladly comply with her wishes."

I straightened out his false ideas of inequality when I learned of his altered financial position, which had seemed a barrier. I also learned that he had felt that his years of squandered opportunity could never make him hope for equal footing as a Christian, but I soon put his mind at ease about equal yoking.

Glyn suggested that we string our relatives and keep them guessing as to our previous attachment. So, it was an interesting voyage which I shall never, never forget as long as I live.

Oh yes, Mr. Pearce. He came up to us, and wished to know my newly found companion. After he had disappeared, Glyn said: "Audrey wrote that you were being driven about quite often by a Mr. Pearce in a large car. Then, when I heard you were accompanying your grandfather with a Mr. Pearce, you seemed lost to me, Lois. I hastened to you when mother's letter assured me you were still 'mine.'"

We parted and I hurried to my cabin to change my dress for late afternoon and evening. Mrs. Forster met me coming out onto the deck and beaming, said, "I wish you to meet my son, Glyn. Glyn, meet a charming young woman who has been very, very kind to me—Lois Stanford."

We shook hands, and Mrs. Forster hurried off and left us to ourselves. How we laughed! Glyn can pull such a poker face! I understand now, so many of his ways when at Bradleholme. He is a perfect actor, and can keep you really guessing what is behind his facial expressions.

Glyn had moved off from me and was leaning over the rail watching the water when grandfather came up. He took this opportunity of making his introductions. "You must meet my granddaughter, Lois Stanford," he said as he drew near to where I was sitting.

"So pleased to make your acquaintance," Glyn said politely, taking my hand.

"Mr. Forster and I became acquainted in London. We had an item of business to transact which brought us into contact with each other frequently," he said, eyeing Glyn. "Now you will pardon me for I want to take my usual walk around the deck."

Mr. Pearce went to his side, and Glyn looked at me, smiling. In the days that followed, we watched these older heads trying to make a match that had long since been made. It was spicing up the voyage for them.

It was my habit to find a sunny spot on deck early in the morning. Here I could read my Bible unmolested as few people were around at that time and Mrs. Forster and Grandfather seldom got about until noon. But as I approached the sunny spot one particular day, Glyn had already preceded me. He looked up, and motioning me to his side said, "Come, Lois, I want you to see my Scripture reading for this morning."

I sat beside him and he handed me his Bible opened at Genesis. "Read it," he said. "I would like to hear it from your lips."

"'It is not good that the man should be alone; I will make him an helpmeet for him.'"

"Now," he said, "skip to the 22nd verse."

"'And the Lord brought her unto the man,'" I read obediently, my face crimsoning.

"The waiting has been worth it all, Lois. It is God Who has brought us together in a most unusual manner. How wonderful it is to abide His perfect timing. How many times I was inclined to complain, and only recently His chastening was upon me sorely. It was then that I saw I had not been perfectly resigned to His will, and, after a struggle, you were given completely into His keeping. We young folks are tempted to want things now, but patience has her perfect work in us when we WAIT. 'They shall not be ashamed that wait for me.'"

Glyn paused and we were both silent as we gazed out at the vastness of the ocean with its numberless waves swelling and then breaking as they reached our vessel. "Tell me, Lois, what the Polisher has taught you as you remained under the discipline of His disc. The marks of His Workmanship are visible upon your countenance. Forgive me for speaking so long about myself."

I told him, Ruth, that the process had been sore, as the cruel disc had ground away the unshapely bits of self-will. Day after day of grinding toil had been mixed with the olive oil of God's comfort and the knowledge that others whom He had loved had gone through the same disciplines. "Let patience have her perfect work, that ye may be perfect and ENTIRE, WANTING NOTHING." Patience had been God's Polisher, and by my "letting" her have her perfect work upon my life, I had wanted nothing.

Remember, Ruth, the time we read together F. B. Meyer's sermon on Abraham? I never did forget how troublesome Ishmael became because Abraham was impatient and thought God was a little slow in fulfilling His promises. At the time, I copied a portion in the back of my Bible. How appropriate it seemed as it was read aloud in the quiet of the early morning:

"Ah, fatal mistake! But how many make it still. They may be true children of God: and yet, in a moment of panic, they will adopt methods of delivering themselves which, to say the least, are questionable; and sow the seeds of sorrow and disaster in after-life, to save themselves from some minor embarrassment. Christian women plunge into the marriage bond with those who are the enemies of God, in order that they may be carried through some financial difficulty. Christian merchants take ungodly partners into business for the sake of the capital they introduce. To enable them to stave off the pressure of difficulties, and to maintain their respectability, Christian people of all grades will court the help of the world. What is this—but going down to Egypt for help?"

"Good," Glyn exclaimed. "I had just marked something in a current religious periodical by A. E. Gould. It's similar, but worth reading, too. We've already begun sharing; looks like we're going to have a rare partnership:

"'To our bustling, "go-getting" age the idea behind 'long-suffering' seems as quaintly out-moded as its sound. To be long-suffering means being willing to wait, for a very long time if need be, without losing one's temper. Many people today don't like to be kept waiting; they expect prompt attention to their needs and wishes, even from God! Paul reminds us that one sign of the presence of the Holy Spirit in human life is this quality of holding out, with patient good humor, when the normal channels by which tension can be relieved are blocked. One of the distinguishing marks of the real Christian is that he is willing to wait for God's time without growing bitter or rebellious. . . . The real test of our worth to the Cause is not merely how we behave when a daring sortie must be made, but how we carry ourselves through the much longer, uneventful periods, suffering what must be endured, sticking it out, as long as the need lasts.'"

Glyn slowly replaced the clipping in the back of his Bible as he said: "An elderly and successful minister once told me that more Christians ruin their lives by wrong timing than rank disobedience. In marriage, it is not so much that they choose the wrong partner, as it is that they are unwilling to wait God's time for their union. Purposes of God are thus frustrated, and both suffer all through their married lives. But, I am assured in our case, God has indeed perfected that which concerned us both. Let's thank Him for this unexpected surprise from His hands."

He drew my hand into his and we bowed our heads close together as he quietly poured out a wealth of love and gratitude to the Savior. It was my first opportunity of seeing Glyn, the former cynical young man, in the role of an ardent Christian. My eyes were brim full when we looked up to find his mother had been standing by. She must have heard part of the prayer. Our secret was out.

"Meet the one who is to become my wife, mother dear," Glyn said. "Aren't you happy?"

"I knew I should eventually find you the right one, Glyn. I was sure this time, I had found one you could love—even you," she said. "But, but, I never dreamed that you would on so brief an acquaintance come to this happy conclusion so quickly. Your father always said when you did find someone to love, you would do so ardently. You two look radiantly happy."

"You see," she went on looking at me, "My son has been extremely hard to please, Miss Stanford. I thought he would be a bachelor for life, and never, never marry. I am ever so happy that I never gave up until I had found the right one."

As she walked happily off, Glyn looked at me. "We shan't tell her our secret. Someone else shall have to break that. She has had so few real pleasures through her life, that I am willing for her to believe that she truly did find you for me."

Mr. Morton and Mrs. Forster soon had their heads together. Grandfather had been quickly apprised of the romance as soon as Mrs. Forster had made her discovery and he was very, very pleased. But seeing that four heads are better than two, we, after much planning and canceling, arranging and disarranging, agreeing and vetoing, finally came to plans regarding the wedding.

CHAPTER TWELVE

THE KING'S OWN SETTING

Lois returned from her ocean cruise, looking a picture of health. I valued our short time together since I was to lose her so soon again. The wedding ceremony was to be performed in London so that friends and relatives of the Stanfords might be able to be present. A second reception was to be held in Africa for the sake of Glyn's relatives and friends.

In spite of Lois's keen desire to keep things extremely simple, Mr. Morton kept adding something until it grew to an elaborate affair. He had robbed himself, through a long-standing grudge, of the joys that being a father and grandfather would naturally have afforded. Mother and daughter, therefore, were anxious to give him the happiness so long withheld, and yielded reluctantly. Mr. Morton had desired a church wedding at his own place of worship, but Larch Memorial Hall stood for so much that was precious in the lives of both Glyn and Lois that it was their natural choice. Rev. Marchant was asked to officiate.

I won't go into detail lest you think that I am unduly interested in wedding ceremonies. After this lovely service and reception, we waved them the happy couple off on a jet plane. I felt a huge lump in my throat and a pain at my heart as I tore myself away from one who had been such a part of my life.

The surprise that awaited Lois in Africa is best told in her own words: "Glyn and I were welcomed at the airport and driven first to his own home. Having met the mother, we were not total strangers. Both of his parents opened their hearts to me, and I felt the warmth of their love. I will try to be to them something of what Kathryn would have been had she lived.

"Oh yes, Ruth, Brenda was there to meet me and she is all and more than Audrey said she was. We are like sisters. The reception was planned at some place a little distance away from Glyn's home, so we motored over there with his parents and Brenda. We drove up to an enclosed settlement of new buildings. A beautiful but strong gate barred our entrance.

"'Only your key will open this gate,' Glyn explained as he assisted me in getting out of the car and stepped with me to the gate. 'Your setting, Lois dear, and your domain.' A little golden lock responded to the key which I had withdrawn from my purse. My eyes scanned the grounds with the drive winding down through flowering shrubs and small trees. Some skilful planner had been at work. Glyn and I walked up the pathway to a new building. It was a small hospital, with additional wings still under construction. Can you imagine my surprise to meet Carey and Dick in the lobby? What a reunion! Dick is to be in charge there.

"Ruth, I feel I am stunned and walking about in a dream. I look at the tall, bronzed, handsome figure by my side and feel the protection and love he offers me, and it is so hard to believe we are man and wife after such long years of anxiety and delay. Still I would not want it otherwise; our appreciation of one another is so great because of the waiting time. I feel ashamed to think that I ever doubted Glyn's faithfulness and love when I see how he had begun to plan immediately he came out here. Every step of this drive gives evidence of a long-sighted planner and reminds me of what my Heavenly Father was doing for me all the while I wondered and questioned.

"We traveled on next to a school building where Carey is to take over until someone else can be engaged. I could write ever so much in detail about all this too. I must go on. Next Glyn showed me a small building with printing equipment and offices for translation and literature distribution work. A few shops, too, are in the process of erection with living accommodation above.

"But Glyn led me proudly to 'our home' last. It is a replica of "Sunny Mount"—every small detail being incorporated—the garden, the gate, the roses and the style of house! Oh, Ruth, how lovely! A garden seat marked the spot representing the one where Glyn first saw me. I was overwhelmed and wanted to inspect every room, but we were due to be at the reception, so reluctantly we left our little home to meet the staff—workers and helpers. In front of a large hall, suitable for services, etc., tables had been arranged and a royal welcome awaited us.

"Afterwards when we were alone, Glyn explained the inspiration for this setting. It was more in keeping than a palatial home, beautiful personal effects, costly jewels, etc., and I learned since that he has placed all his capital into this center for the promotion of Christ's Name. What a marvelous setting! A beautiful oil painting portraying a head of Christ, set in a marvelous diamond, occupies a large place in our lounge. Underneath the picture are the words, 'The Perfect Gem.' Hand in hand we dedicated our united love, strength, energies, and talents to presenting Him to needy men and women everywhere. To them He is 'a root out of dry ground'; to us He is the 'altogether lovely One' and we wish to present Him in such a way that His dazzling beauty may captivate others as it has us."

*** *** * * * * * *

Several years have elapsed since the wedding now. Friends have joined them in their work. Amyenne Manvers, who took a nursing course, is out working as a Sister in their hospital. Nata has married a young doctor and is ministering in a mission hospital elsewhere abroad. Pauline has found another partner, and is laboring earnestly for the salvation of the city dwellers. Judith and her two children attend Larch Memorial Hall, and every now and again she gives a hand to the work there.

Audrey Castleton became Mrs. Ashleford. Mrs. Melvern soon discovered the duplicity of her brilliant helper after Judith had made her apology. The tragedy of Audrey's life is that with her brilliant mind the possibilities and usefulness and happiness seemed unlimited. By choosing her own way, and subtly planning her own life, she missed the best. She is hidden away in some obscure corner of the world, still intriguing and planning, but out of tune with the Infinite and so not fitting into His world purpose.

Mrs. Stanford, still not too vigorous and active, lives with her old father, but she is able to act the part of intercessor for her children who are doing the work she had so loved in earlier days. And I have been invited out to Africa to continue my own work there. Lois and Glyn have a baby boy which gladdens the hearts of his parents and promises to be much the image of his father. These two have not forgotten their search for diamonds in the rough, to be presented at that Great Day to the Master, as a part of His great jewel collection. And if they needs must work with graphite in the rough, they know a supernatural agency which transmutes this raw material into gems of priceless worth.

The Velvet Curtain

Leaving the Iron Curtain behind forever, Esther has no idea that she has merely exhcanged one Curtain for another...

Step back into the eighties when Communism still held deadly sway in Eastern Europe and imagine yourself with Esther, a Romanian teenager, coming to America, the land of freedom, for the first time and discovering that there is much more awaiting her than a mere change of cultures.

Her beauty and individuality attract the attention of handsome Ron Atwood and her talent as a singer soon opens up a whole new world. She rejoices in her new-found liberty and popularity but the "curtain" that her elderly friend, Hugh Gardner, warns her about in the plane is fast closing in. Will it completely smother her, or will she be able to escape its folds?

by,
Trudy Harvey Tait
336 page paperback
Size: 5.5 x 8.5 in.
ISBN: 1-932774-69-6

Behind The Velvet Curtain

This book, a sequel to The Velvet Curtain, continues the story of Esther and Gabby, the two Romanian girls who, escape the Iron Curtain, only to find themselves enmeshed in its Western counterpart. Esther takes drastic measures to stay clear of the Velvet Curtain while Gabby denies its very existence and calls it, instead, The American Dream.

And yet, behind this all-enveloping Curtain, the two girls and their friends, Len and Ron Atwood, discover that God can turn tragedy into triumph. The story will take unexpected twists and turns as His grace invades, transforms, and redirects the lives of flawed and erring human beings.

by,
Trudy Harvey Tait
304 page paperback
Size: 5.5 x 8.5 inches
ISBN: 1-978-932774-70-2

Escaping The Velvet Curtain

by,
Trudy Harvey Tait
271 page paperback
Size: 5.5 x 8.5 inches
ISBN: 978-1-932774-71-9

Escaping The Velvet Curtain continues the saga of Esther, her sister Gabby, and their friends.

Exploring the various ways in which each of them seek to escape the Velvet Curtain has made me retrace my own spiritual pilgrimage. I realize afresh that God puts us in a seemingly impossible position and then delights to deliver us when He sees that our trust is in Him alone.

Love Me & Let Me Go

by Trudy Harvey Tait

This is a novel but, like many novels, is inspired by personal experience and observation. It is set in the 1970's and centers around the heroine's struggle to find her own spiritual feet while still locked in step with her very devoted, very sincere, and very controlling father. She adores, respects, and fears him, and yet she longs to discover her own voice--be her own person. This involves choosing where she will worship, what she will do with her life, the type of man she wants to marry. And, eventually, she does all this, but at what price! "Love me and let me go!: she pleads with those who love her best. And when they, very reluctantly, do just that, she discovers, in the end, that true spiritual freedom is only found through capitulating to the will of God.

Author: Trudy Harvey Tait
Number of pages: 268
ISBN: 978-1-932774-
Type: paperback
Size: 5.5 x 8.5 inches

www.ingramcontent.com/pod-product-compliance
Lightning Source LLC
LaVergne TN
LVHW090955080826
845145LV00003B/1017

* 9 7 8 1 9 3 2 7 7 4 0 6 1 *